"I'd like to interview you sometime, Officer Harris," Courtney said.

"Tradition dictates that policemen and reporters have trouble getting along," Mike pointed out.

"I'm not much of a traditionalist. How about you?"

"I am...most of the time." He smiled. "But I'm easily influenced."

"Good. I admire a man whose mind can be changed. How about doing that interview right now?"

It was the story she was after, Courtney reminded herself when she found him staring into her eyes. Never mind the fact that the man filled the entire apartment with his presence.

"Well," he offered, "I am off duty."

Mike was pleased with the prospect of having more time to study this woman he'd rescued. He was still wondering what it was about her that had captivated him the other night. The memory of holding her in his arms had stayed with him far longer than it should for a professional man like himself....

Dear Reader,

Spellbinders! That's what we're striving for. The editors at Silhouette are determined to capture your imagination and win your heart with every single book we publish. Each month, six Special Editions are chosen with *you* in mind.

Our authors are our inspiration. Writers such as Nora Roberts, Tracy Sinclair, Kathleen Eagle, Carole Halston and Linda Howard—to name but a few—are masters at creating endearing characters and heartrending love stories. Their characters are everyday people—just like you and me—whose lives have been touched by love, whose dreams and desires suddenly come true!

So find a cozy, quiet place to read, and create your own special moment with a Silhouette Special Edition.

Sincerely,

The Editors
SILHOUETTE BOOKS

PAULA HAMILTON
The Man
Behind the Badge

Silhouette Special Edition

Published by Silhouette Books New York

America's Publisher of Contemporary Romance

SILHOUETTE BOOKS
300 East 42nd St., New York, N.Y. 10017

Copyright © 1987 by Paula Hamilton

ISBN: 0-373-09400-0

First Silhouette Books printing August 1987

Books by Paula Hamilton

Silhouette Special Edition

Dream Lover #340
In the Name of Love #382
The Man Behind the Badge #400

PAULA HAMILTON

shares the basic characteristics of all writers—an insatiable curiosity and a deep love of books. She lives with her husband and two daughters on the edge of the Texas hill country, and when she isn't writing she may be found reading, golfing or trying to keep up with her busy family activities. She tries to begin each day with the intention of living life to the fullest and says the best way to do that is with lots of laughter.

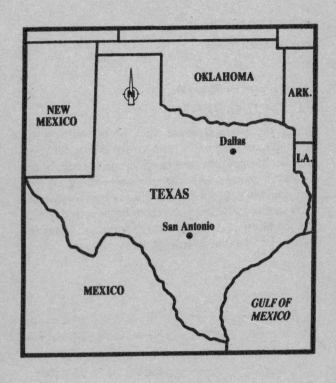

Prologue

Hold it!''

Some instinctive reaction made Courtney Evans's blood run cold when she heard the hostile words shouted close behind her. But that same reaction made her drop her umbrella and run. She didn't know exactly what was happening, but through the rain she could see her apartment building and its welcoming lights only a little way down the sidewalk.

Caught from behind before she had gone more than a few feet, she lost her balance and found herself falling toward the pavement. Powerful arms clutched her midsection, holding her upright, and she fleetingly thought that her chest might be crushed.

The stranger's dirty fingers clamped down hard over her mouth, preventing her from screaming. Her eyes watered, and she felt her legs begin to quake.

"Come any closer and I'll kill her," the man who held her hard against his side shouted at two policemen who watched, their revolvers aimed helplessly at Courtney.

The inky rain poured down on them, chilling the early-October evening even more. One of the thoughts that flashed through Courtney's mind was that this night might be her last. She was overwhelmed with the sudden knowledge that she might die, and she was terrified. At the age of twenty-eight, she'd given only minimal thought to her mortality—until now.

Her eyes widened in shock. With each word he'd screamed, the man had tightened his viselike grip. The pain in her ribs was now so excruciating that she desperately gasped for breath.

"Listen, fella, take it easy."

A police car had pulled up to the curb, and a man in a trench coat had gotten out. He was the one speaking now, his calm voice strangely out of place. Courtney watched him edge closer, his arms opened in a conciliatory gesture.

Still gasping for breath, she glanced around frantically. From where she stood, in the arms of this maniac, she could see the entrance to her apartment less than a hundred yards away.

Courtney moved instinctively, and then knew she shouldn't have. The stranger shoved a cold, hard gunbarrel against her temple.

"I ain't kidding. Another step and she's had it!"

The man cocked his gun, and the noise reverberated through Courtney's skull. Trembling, she tried to shut her eyes, but was unable to keep them closed. When and if anything happened, she wanted to know it. It might be her last experience on earth.

"Whatever the problem is, we can work it out without the woman." Again the man in the trench coat spoke, and as he did, he took another step forward.

Courtney held her breath. Her future, she knew, rested in this man's hands now. She watched and listened, trying to remember the words to a prayer.

The man was still talking, encouraging Courtney's attacker to let her go. He took another step toward them.

Listen to the man, she wanted to shout. She felt the pressure against her ribs ease a little as the man in the trench coat kept talking, his voice hypnotic, soothing. Courtney wondered whether he was having any effect on the violent stranger.

Suddenly, as quickly as it had begun, it was over. The sound of metal hitting concrete was music to Courtney's ears.

Abruptly set free, she was thrown back against the wall of the nearby building. Wiping the rain from her eyes with shaking hands, she watched the stranger being handcuffed and led away.

"Are you all right?" The man in the trench coat hurried toward her.

A flood of relief washed over her, and with it came the urge to throw herself into her savior's arms. When she did, a feeling of absolute safety engulfed her, making her cling tightly to her rescuer and wallow in the strength of his embrace.

Finally she came to her senses and took a cautious step backward. "I'm all right," she said with a series of jerky nods.

Taking her solicitously by the arm, the man in the trench coat began leading her away from the scene of her ordeal.

"I'll see you safely home."

Chapter One

On the Thursday night after Courtney's ordeal, she answered a knock at her apartment door. With a caution born of her recent experience, she kept the chain lock secured and opened the door a crack.

"Hello, Miss Evans. May I come in?"

Courtney gasped when she saw who it was, and with trembling fingers she unlatched the chain and pulled the door open. "Certainly," she said, trying to conceal the effect her visitor had on her. She hadn't anticipated seeing her rescuer ever again.

"I just stopped by to let you know that the man captured the other night was wanted for murder and armed robbery in Oklahoma. He's being extradited."

"That's good news," she said, looking up into the tall man's dark eyes.

It occurred to her then that this man intended to stay. He was looking around, studying the foyer, studying her, as if he were investigating the scene of a crime.

Without thinking, she grabbed for the trench coat he handed her. When he gazed expectantly into the apartment, she smiled and led him down the narrow hallway lined with photographs. When they were standing in the middle of her living room, she turned to face him, wondering what else he wanted and why she felt so strangely uncomfortable in his presence.

"Do you have any coffee? It's been a long day," he said, making himself comfortable.

"Instant."

Did all policemen take control like this? she wondered. Since the moment he'd stepped inside her apartment, wearing his authority like a shield, she'd automatically responded to his unspoken commands.

There seemed to be expectation on his part. There was doubt on hers.

"Instant's fine."

He watched her walk away from him, and he thought about how much stronger she seemed than she had the other night. At the time he'd felt a rare surge of protectiveness for her. Now he wondered what it was about the woman that had triggered such a response. In a big-city police department like his, officers became callous toward criminals and victims alike.

"Does this mean that that man's going to be gone for good?" she called from the kitchen as she made two steaming cups of coffee.

"The odds are that he'll be tried in Oklahoma first."

Courtney walked into the living room carrying two mugs of hot coffee on a bamboo tray and served him first. "I'm glad to know he's leaving the state." She took hers and stirred in half a package of artificial sweetener. Then, before she drank it, she brushed away an unruly strand of black hair that had escaped from behind her ear.

"I figured you might be. That's why I came by to tell you."

She watched him as he settled back against the thick peach cushions on the rattan sofa and drank his coffee. For days she'd been thinking about him until she wondered if she was becoming obsessed. She'd daydreamed about him, and she'd resented herself for doing it.

Why? That was the million-dollar question. She reminded herself that he was a policeman, and that she wanted nothing to do with a man who wore a badge. Part of her, however, had other ideas, ideas about a virile man, one who was handsome, whose arms had engulfed her and held her safe. The man had, after all, saved her life.

"About that night, Mr. Harris..."

"Call me Mike."

She had already decided that his voice would be hard to forget. Firm, authoritative, but gentle, he sounded as if he would prove to be a fair and impartial man. That certainly wasn't her view of all policemen.

"Okay, Mike. I want to thank you. I was terribly upset that night, and when you brought me home I didn't tell you how much I appreciated what you did."

He tilted his head toward her and smiled understandingly. "It's all part of the job. No thanks are necessary."

Resisting the urge to say that for some in his profession his statement wasn't at all true, she answered, "I think they are."

There now, she said to herself. You've done what any well-mannered young woman should. You've said your thanks. Now see what he has on his mind and escort him to the door.

Before she said anything, though, Courtney began to wonder if this house call was strictly business. Surely he could have relayed his information by telephone far more easily than by paying her a visit.

She studied the dark brown eyes that had seemed so perceptive the other night, and the ruggedly

handsome face. Had he come for purely professional reasons, she asked herself. Or did he have
something more on his mind?

"I'm just glad things turned out the way they
did," Mike said.

He wasn't accustomed to gratitude, and that
wasn't what he'd come for. It made him uneasy to
have someone thank him for something he did as
part of his job.

"I am, too," she said quietly, wondering for the
hundredth time how long it would take before she
would forget how frightened she had been. It was a
first for her: the first time she'd thought she might
die.

He put down his mug and took another quick
glance around the small living room. Maybe his
coming here hadn't been such a good idea.

This was a completely new experience for him, and
he didn't know exactly what to do. He'd never before wanted to ask anyone he'd met through his job
for a date.

He'd acted on impulse. Normally methodical to a
fault, Mike now realized he had acted without
thinking things through.

"Time to go," he said abruptly, and stood.
"Thanks for the coffee."

"You're welcome," Courtney said, following him
to the door, staring up at his broad shoulders as she
walked.

And then the thought struck her that in her surprise at seeing him here she'd forgotten to take advantage of the moment. A good reporter always kept her job uppermost in her mind, she reminded herself.

"I'm very interested in your profession, Mike," she said eagerly. "I'd like to know more about police negotiators."

He smiled again, but this time his smile lit up his face, softening the hard-bitten look she'd first seen the other night when he'd watched the man being led away. "I'm a reporter," she said, as if to justify her curiosity.

"A reporter?"

"Yes, and since I profited from your talents . . ." Her voice trailed off, then picked up steam again. "I'm embarking on a series about law enforcement. I'd like to interview you sometime."

"I don't know," he responded cautiously. "Cops and reporters usually have trouble getting along." When he spoke, a frown creased his brow. He was serious.

Her first inclination was to agree heartily, but Courtney was intent upon putting him at ease. "I think we've gotten along pretty well so far. How about you?"

He smiled. "Now that you mention it, we have."

"Good. Say, how about doing that interview right now, this evening? I've got my tape recorder, and I

THE MAN BEHIND THE BADGE

could offer you a second cup of coffee while the water's still hot.''

"I'd better not," he said cautiously.

"Are you sure you wouldn't like to stay?" Courtney blurted out before she even realized what she was saying. "I'm really interested in hearing about your work." It was the story she was after, she reminded herself when she found herself staring into his eyes. Never mind the fact that the man filled the entire apartment with his presence. Remember that he's a policeman.

He felt a moment's pleasure at the way she'd taken the initiative and asked him to stay. He wanted nothing more than to do as she'd asked, but he hesitated, looking down at his watch.

"Come on. Just a few minutes. Then you can go."

"Well," he offered. "I am off duty now."

"Good."

Mike sat down again and waited while she went into the kitchen for the coffee. He was happy to be staying, pleased with the prospect of having more time to study this woman who'd been on his mind for days. He was still wondering what it was about her that had so captivated him the other night. He'd felt as if he were a knight rescuing a fair maiden, and the memory of the way she'd collapsed in his arms had stayed with him far longer than it should have. He'd handled hundreds of cases every bit as dangerous, but never before had he been attracted to any of the people he'd rescued.

She had shoulder-length black hair and bangs that swept across her forehead. He thought she might be Irish, or possibly English, with a rose-toned complexion that made her look as if she were eternally blushing. He'd never seen eyes as pale a blue as hers; they were captivating.

"Here we are," Courtney said when she returned with his coffee.

"Thanks."

"You're quite welcome." She put her mug down, and he watched the graceful way she moved, each action smooth and sure. Mike guessed her height to be about five-three, nearly a foot shorter than he was.

"So what would you like to know about the police business?" he asked politely, already trying to decide the best way to describe his work. It seemed everyone wanted to know what it was like to be a police negotiator.

"Like how you got into the job. Why you chose it. Why you stay with it. The usual."

He studied her again, his eyes wide and analytical. "I don't know if I'm ready for all that right now."

"Too much, huh?" She gave him what she hoped would pass for a playful grin, then picked up her mug.

If there was anything Courtney was good at, it was using her charms to gain interviews. She had a great deal of experience, and seldom lost a good opportunity. Now that she had her shot at this interview, she was determined not to blow it.

"Yeah." He looked at his watch again. "Say, have you had dinner?"

"No, why?" It was only seven o'clock, and Courtney often didn't eat until late in the evening, after she had all her work finished for the night.

"I was thinking we could go down on the Riverwalk and get something to eat. I've been on duty for twelve hours straight, and I'm starving."

"Well, I . . ."

"Come on. Put on your raincoat, and let's go. If you're really interested, I'll answer all the questions you can think of."

His face had brightened up when he smiled. Gone was the brooding, secretive expression that seemed to be his stock-in-trade. He looked years younger now, younger and happier.

She looked up into his dark brown eyes, and suddenly she felt pulled in vastly different directions. The reporter in her said "Go" because she might get something out of him for her articles. The woman who'd watched her sister suffer through a brutal excuse for a marriage with a policeman said "Kick the bum out." And the feminine side of her said "This man is attracted to you. See how he studies you, see how absorbed in you he is.''

''Give me a second,'' she said, full of misgivings.

She went down the hallway, shaking her head. *If anyone in your family could see you now, Courtney,* she said to herself. *Going out with a policeman.*

When she returned from the bedroom, she was without her coat. ''I forgot I took it to the cleaners.'' She smiled. ''Oh, well, I don't need it anyway. It's not raining.''

''But it looks like it might.'' He didn't want her to get cold. Her slacks and short-sleeved yellow blouse didn't look at all warm.

''I'll be fine,'' she insisted.

''Okay, if you're sure. I was thinking about walking down to the Lone Star Cafe. How does that sound to you?'' He led her out the door, checking the lock as they went. He gave her a quick smile, then possessively took her arm and led the way.

''I'll go wherever you want. I'm really excited about getting an interview with you. You could be a key part of my articles.''

They walked down the sidewalk along the San Antonio River. Mike was envying her the pleasure of living right in the heart of the downtown area.

''Where do you work, Courtney?''

She was concentrating on keeping up with him. His long, loose but rhythmic strides almost forced her to jog.

"For the *San Antonio Light*. I go to night school at St. Mary's," she continued, a note of pride in her voice. "I'm studying law."

"That accounts for the textbooks I saw on your bedside table."

She blinked, then looked at him questioningly. "When did you see my bedside table?"

"Hey." He laughed, trying to dispel her sudden tension. "I'm a policeman, remember? I glanced in at your bedroom when I first came into your apartment." He waited for it to sink in. "It's a professional habit. Observation. Deduction. You know."

"Oh," she said quietly.

He tempered his next comment with a mischievous grin. "I could tell you some other things about yourself that I've observed..." He changed his mind, and dismissed the idea with a wave of his hand. It smacked of intimate conversation, and he was afraid that might frighten her off.

He did know a great deal about her already. He'd read her info sheet, the one he had filled out the night of the incident.

He knew she had never been married, and he'd known where she worked before she'd told him. The other things he'd read about her he wanted to hear her tell him. Now he was figuring her for a jogger. She had picked up the jogging pace again, that steady sort of rhythm, and in front of them he could see the sign hanging out over the river advertising the Lone Star Cafe.

She gave him a look of apprehension before speaking. "So much has happened lately—things so out of the ordinary—that it bothered me there for a minute. You know, the idea that someone knew something about me that I hadn't told him." She smiled slightly. "Guess I'm still a little jumpy."

"Of course. Crime victims like yourself go through a great many experiences after being attacked. Are you afraid now?"

"Not really...except when I walk by the spot where that man grabbed me. I find myself looking all around before hurrying on." She took a deep breath, remembering. "I still think about how I didn't even hear him come up behind me."

"The fear is not at all unusual, and don't worry, it will pass." They walked up the stone steps to the café. "Would you like to sit out here on the balcony or go inside?"

Mike let go of her arm and moved his hand up around her shoulders with a gentle authority. Although it was merely a friendly gesture, she couldn't help but acknowledge a certain response that was tingling its way up her spine. That was all part of his role, she told herself. She looked up at him to see if she could guess what he was thinking, but his expression was unreadable as he waited for her to make up her mind.

"Any other time I'd say let's eat out here, but it's a little chilly, don't you think?" It must be chilly, Courtney told herself; she was shivering slightly.

He nodded. "A typical Texas October. It'll probably rain." He told the waiter where they'd like to sit, choosing a window table that would allow them a decent view of the river, and then politely held the chair for her.

Courtney was impressed by his take-charge attitude and his old-world manners. She had to admit that in Mike Harris they were two very attractive traits.

The Lone Star Cafe faced a main street only a few blocks from the Alamo, and it backed up against the San Antonio River. Along the river's edge were two enormous cypress trees which afforded shade year-round. Inside the restaurant was a massive oak bar, surrounded on three sides by small painted tables. The service was less than perfect, but the casual atmosphere was always pleasant, even on a cloudy night such as this one.

After they'd ordered, Mike said, "I like your photographs."

"Which photographs?"

"The ones hanging in the hall."

"Family." She shook her head. "You're the most observant man I've ever met."

"Part of the job."

"Photography's part of mine, but it's also a hobby. Every reporter has to be a passable photographer in addition to everything else. The way a policeman is required to know how to fire a gun, I suppose." Her gaze traveled down to his chest. "Where's yours?"

"Gun? I don't wear it when I'm off duty."

Memories of her sister came to mind. "I always figured that was part of it...the image...the gun as some sort of symbol and all. You know, the invincible look."

He caught the anger in her voice and wondered what could have caused it.

"Is that the way you see us, concerned with authoritarian images?"

"Isn't that—" She stopped herself. It would do no good for her to tell him what she really thought. Not if she wanted the interview he'd promised.

Courtney changed tactics, returning to the conversation they'd had on their walk. "I meant what I said earlier. Your job fascinates me." She chose her next words carefully. "I'm going to be doing a ten-part series on the police in the city, and so help me, I never thought about a police negotiator."

"No reason you should," he replied, shrugging as if trying to downplay the importance she was giving him and his job.

"I disagree. After hearing your voice, the way you handled that man ... It takes skill."

"Many people could do the same thing."

"Are you a clinical psychologist?"

Their chicken-fried steaks were delivered, enormous patties swamped in country gravy. Courtney seasoned hers as she waited for his reply.

"Naw." He shook his head slowly. "The truth of the matter is this, Courtney. In most big cities the person who has my job has a doctorate in psychology and a fistful of diplomas. I'm a product of the old school—the school of experience." He took a bite of his steak and swallowed it before he went on. "I was just a police detective who stumbled on a couple of cases where I had to do some fast talking. I was lucky; everything worked out pretty well, and all of a sudden some of your fellow reporters labeled me a police negotiator. The department brass liked it, thought it was good PR, so I was stuck with the job. Now I have a heavier work load than ever."

There was something in his voice that disturbed her. He sounded bored, drained, as though the job was something he almost resented. For the first time she took notice of the strands of gray hair at his temples and the lines by his eyes, and she wondered about him.

"Is this a follow-up you came to do? Reassurance for the crime victim?"

His eyes met hers. "Yes."

"That's why you came to see me tonight?"

"Yes." Again he looked at her intently.

Why she felt disappointed by his answer she couldn't say, except perhaps that her vanity had made her think he'd come for personal reasons. She looked down at her plate, uncomfortably aware of the way he was watching her.

There was such a vitality in this man. His entire being seemed acutely aware of everything. He was alert and cautious, like a hunter, and above all, he was strikingly male.

The reporter in her spoke, "Why don't you let me do an exclusive article on you? Separate from my series."

She wondered what he'd say if he knew that the ten-part report she was working on would be less than favorable in its judgment of the police.

"Why don't you finish your steak, and we'll order the fresh-baked apple pie?" he countered.

Seeing that he wasn't going to talk about himself any more, she let the conversation die. But her interest wasn't dampened. It was more fired up than ever.

As he ate, he watched her. Maybe he'd made a mistake in contacting her, but she'd stirred something in him the other night that hadn't been touched in a long time—too long a time.

But right now he was on the edge of burnout in his job and was considering a career change. He didn't want to involve himself with anything else. And besides all that, there was something in her attitude that disturbed him. He wasn't sure she meant what she said. Either she found him distasteful or she was carrying a grudge of some sort or maybe she didn't like policemen.

She was being nice to him because she wanted an interview, but there was something else to it as well. Mike was sure he was right.

After they finished eating, they headed back down the Riverwalk toward her apartment building. The air was cooler than it had been earlier, and before they'd gone very far it began to rain.

The cold rain soaked through Courtney's clothes so fast that she began to shiver. She crossed her arms and began walking quickly to keep warm.

Mike glanced at her, and before she knew what was happening he'd stripped off his sports coat and thrown it over her shoulders. "Thanks," she said. "But now you'll get soaked."

"It's not far," Mike told her. He put his arm around her as they ran through the streets.

When they reached the apartment she invited him in. "I could give you another cup of coffee to take off the chill. Besides, we didn't get very far with my interview," she added, hoping she hadn't missed her chance.

He was soaked to the skin. His wet hair looked even darker than usual and was beginning to curl slightly. His shirt clung to his skin, revealing a muscular torso. She wondered if he worked out with weights or if he'd just been blessed with that body.

"Another time," he replied. "I'd better be going." He took his jacket from her and slipped it back over his own shoulders.

She watched him dress, feeling vaguely annoyed at herself. Why was she so uncomfortably aware of him as a man? It had always been so easy for Courtney to maintain a professional detachment from all her interview subjects, but something about Mike destroyed that detachment, made her want to get far closer to him than she ought to. Even the simple act of putting on his jacket seemed strangely fascinating to her. For a woman who a few hours earlier had been reluctant to allow him into her house, who'd spent the evening trying to convince him to give her an interview, she found herself paying far too much attention to the way he looked, to his every move.

"You're welcome. It was nice to have company for a change. I usually end up eating by myself."

She wanted to ask him why, but she held back. He probably already thought she asked too many questions, and she was concerned that she might sound more like a woman who wanted to know about the man than a reporter who wanted to know about the policeman.

"Good night, Courtney."

Mike nodded his head toward her. For a moment they looked at one another in frank mutual assessment. His gaze traveled down to her toes and back again, finally settling on her face.

His brooding appraisal started a tremor deep within her. There was an awareness between them as they stood staring at one another, an awareness that was very disturbing.

Then, with a brief smile, he turned and walked back to the waiting elevators.

Chapter Two

"Say, Courtney, I heard you had a little excitement the other night." Mary Claire Ferguson, another reporter for the *Light*, stood beside Courtney's desk, eating her first doughnut of the morning and sipping the first of many cups of coffee she'd buy from the food wagon.

Courtney nodded as she sipped her own coffee. "You just now heard? I figured everybody knew all about that days ago." She shook her head playfully. "And to think that you of all people missed it."

The night shift was leaving, and the daytime employees had just come on duty. There was the usual hum of people talking, telephones ringing and computer printers running.

"Yeah, and I can't believe it. What did you think was actually happening to you the moment that slimy guy grabbed you?" Mary Claire took another big bite of her doughnut while she waited for Courtney's reply.

Courtney gathered her thoughts, pleased that Mary Claire seemed interested. Before Osgood Merriweather came between them they'd been inseparable, and Courtney missed the closeness of their friendship. Mary Claire had been the only person in the world Courtney could open up to. Now their conversations were usually superficial, sometimes even strained.

Once upon a time she'd kept Mary Claire from overdosing on doughnuts, while Mary Claire had kept her from getting wrapped up in every new cause that came along. They were very different. Mary Claire loved the opera. Courtney flipped over rock and roll. Mary Claire wore dress-for-success business suits, while Courtney favored casual clothes like linen skirts and blouses. Mary Claire didn't believe in involving herself with too many things at once. She kept her distance. Courtney always threw herself into things with a vengeance. When Courtney first met Mary Claire, she'd found her reserved and shy. Courtney had changed her for a while, making her see the bright side of things, the positive side.

Now she worried that, without her, Mary Claire might be sliding back into her old habits.

Courtney giggled nervously. "I thought about the fact that I might actually die, right then and there. That it might be all over for me."

"Gad. It must have been frightening." Mary Claire shuddered a little and took another bite.

"Having a gun shoved against your head can be a little frightening, all right." Courtney could still almost feel the cold metal of the gun every time she thought about the incident.

Mary Claire finished off her doughnut and rubbed her fingers together to dispose of the sugary crumbs.

"Well, maybe there's one positive thing that will come out of all of this. Maybe you could use the experience in an article someday."

"Yeah, that's one way to look at it." Courtney nodded and watched Mary Claire walk to her own desk, coffee cup in hand.

Mary Claire couldn't know it, but Courtney thought something good had already come of the experience: she'd met Mike Harris. And she was convinced that the man was an absolute godsend for her series of articles on local law enforcement.

Now that she'd had time to assess the situation, she'd realized why she'd been so caught up with him the evening before. She knew that the reason for her overwhelming attraction to him was that he'd rescued her, saved her from the hands of death. Any psychologist would agree with her, Courtney thought. It was a natural reaction to a traumatic situation.

That explained why she'd daydreamed about him, why she'd found herself enjoying his company the evening before and why her pulse rate seemed to increase whenever she came close to him. Those feelings existed, she told herself, only because Mike had been the man to come to her aid. He'd been her savior.

She would never have found him appealing if they'd met under any other circumstances, particularly since she didn't care for policemen in general.

She wondered if she would hear from him again. If she didn't, she'd have to contact him to get her interview. She'd be gracious, of course, but this time she'd be strictly professional, now that she'd cleared her head and knew exactly what she was after.

"Good morning, Courtney." Osgood Merriweather, a fellow reporter, was getting a drink from the water fountain about three feet from her desk.

"Good morning, Osgood." She gave him the briefest of glances and went back to proofreading her text.

"I tried to call you last night, but you were out," Osgood said, nervously adjusting his hairpiece.

"Yes, I was." Courtney had learned not to give Osgood any information about herself. It only served to encourage him.

Osgood Merriweather was typical of the guys Courtney was always having to say no to. He was nice, too nice. A girl could go crazy listing his virtues. He was clean, honest and dependable. Courtney smiled as she realized that her description would just as easily fit a used car on a dealer's lot, but that was the way she perceived Osgood.

"I had been hoping to come over," he complained.

Osgood worshiped Courtney. He would be perfectly willing **to** be her slave. He'd said so many times. And the man was unusually persistent. No matter how many times she refused his invitations for dates, he continued to ask her. Osgood just didn't give up.

"I'm sorry, Osgood. I've been very busy lately. Why don't you call Mary Claire instead?" She watched his expression as it went from bright to gloomy.

Osgood had cost her Mary Claire's friendship. It was a terrible triangle. Osgood wanted Courtney. Mary Claire wanted Osgood. Courtney wanted nothing more than to be rid of him and to have her friend back.

"Sooner or later, you've got to be able to squeeze me into your busy schedule."

Once again he tapped his hairpiece. He couldn't keep his hands off it, making it even more conspicuous than it had to be.

Courtney smiled at him, hoping she hadn't hurt his feelings. The man was very nice. And he wasn't unattractive. He certainly had the potential to be quite good-looking, she thought. But he was too formal. That was part of the problem. He never lost control, never went wild, never gave her any indication that he'd be fun in any way.

"Excuse me, Osgood. I have to get this proofed and back downstairs." She picked up her reading glasses and put them on as she went back to studying her copy.

"I'll see you a little bit later," Osgood said before returning to his office.

She listened to him walking away. It was almost incomprehensible to Courtney that a man like Osgood could be the excellent reporter that he was. In her opinion, she was good at the job because she had all the right traits. She was inquisitive, interested, concerned, unflappable and stubborn enough to stick to her guns. Osgood had none of those characteristics, yet he was good at his job.

Maybe the real problem was that he reminded her of her ex-boyfriend, Tom. An accountant, Tom had spent his days counting his boss's money and his nights counting his own and Courtney's. He was always telling her how she should budget her money. He'd made a federal case out of the most trivial things, and Courtney had eventually discovered the only thing he loved was himself.

The experience had taught her a lesson. She didn't want any deep commitments in the near future, and any man she ended up dating would have to be loads of fun. She'd had it with overly serious men.

Serious men usually kept their emotions under lock and key. Like Tom, they were almost completely unable to express their needs and their feelings. She was looking for a man who'd talk, who'd share himself with her. She just wasn't suited to men like Osgood Merriweather. Courtney had learned that the hard way.

And neither was she suited to a man like Mike Harris, she told herself. After her sister Chris's experience married to a policeman who took out his rage and frustration on her, Courtney had sworn she'd never get emotionally involved with a man who wore a badge. Yet she still couldn't completely forget how attracted she'd been to Mike the other evening. No matter how much she tried to discount those feelings, they still disturbed her.

On Thursday night, when Courtney was at law school, the discussion centered around the fine line the nation's police were required to follow concerning citizens' rights. As the discussion became more interesting and varied, Courtney mentioned the fact that she had recently met a police negotiator.

"Courtney, I think the class could benefit from hearing someone like that speak. Do you think you could get this officer to come to class one evening for a discussion?''

Wishing she had never opened her mouth, Courtney looked at her professor. ''No, sir. I don't think so.''

''Why not? It could be a very profitable experience for the whole class,'' the professor said in a most intimidating manner.

''Yes, I know, but—''

''Come on, Courtney. It relates perfectly to what we're studying now,'' a fellow student, who was always working on brownie points, said.

''Unless, of course, you prefer to keep your relationship with this police negotiator strictly personal.'' The professor arched his brows high.

Courtney blushed. ''No, sir. Not at all.''

''Then . . . ?'' he said expectantly.

''Then I'll call him right away.''

Nodding to her as if to say she'd wasted far too much of his precious time, the professor said to the class, ''Let's all be prepared with questions we might want this fellow to answer.''

As soon as Courtney got home that night, even though it was ten o'clock, she called Mike, grateful that he had a listed number.

The moment Mike heard her voice, his internal struggle began again. He was captivated by her, but he told himself he hadn't wanted to hear from her.

"Mike, I was wondering if it would be possible for you to come to my law class at St. Mary's and speak to the group about your work as a police negotiator?"

How many times in the last few days had he thought about her? he asked himself. Too many.

She was giving him the perfect opportunity to pick up on the tentative relationship they had begun. He'd accompany her to her class. Afterward they'd go out for a bite to eat or a cup of coffee. They'd talk. He'd ask her out again. The possibilities were limitless.

But he couldn't do it.

"Thanks, Courtney. It sounds very interesting, but I can't. I'm busy with a case right now, and there's no time left over for anything else." He unintentionally emphasized the word "anything."

"Oh, well, anytime would be all right with us. We meet two nights a week for the entire semester," she said.

"I can't promise you anything," he told her, realizing how true his words were. That was why he wouldn't, couldn't, see her again. He couldn't promise anyone anything at all.

"Oh, I see," she said, in a voice that told him she didn't see at all.

"I appreciate your asking, though." He tried to ease the rejection a little.

"Yeah, sure," she replied. "Well, I'll let you go."

When she hung up, Mike sat staring at the telephone, feeling like a heel. The lady deserved better.

He closed his eyes. He'd met Courtney by sheer accident, and he hadn't been able to get her out of his mind since he first saw her. Going to her apartment had been the most unprofessional thing he'd done in a long time.

And it had been a mistake.

Courtney Evans was bright, fresh, interesting and interested in everything. She was like daylight to his nighttime. That was the problem right there. A guy who was suffering from burnout, on the verge of quitting his job and leaving everything behind, was no good for a vivacious woman like Courtney.

He looked around the room, taking in the crowded bookshelves, the dhurrie he'd bought because its pale tones blended well with his white modern sofa, and the many other objects that had once been so important to him. Even here, in the house he'd bought and reworked with his own hands, everything seemed dismal and depressing. It was as if all the life had gone from the place.

He picked up his latest copy of *Texas Monthly* and tried to read the first article he came to, but it was no use.

The telephone rang again, and Mike sprang to answer it before it could ring twice. "Hello," he said with a characteristically impatient tone in his voice.

"Hi." Her voice sang across the wire. "It's me again."

This time he was unable to resist. A man can only hold off so long, he said to himself, shaking his head.

"Hi, Courtney. Long time no hear."

She laughed, a high melodious sound. "Yeah. I figured I didn't try hard enough on the last call, so I should give it the old college try one more time. If you knew my professor you'd understand my insistence. He'll remember this come grading time." She was still having trouble believing she'd actually got herself into this, but she was going to do everything within her power to make sure Mike Harris appeared before her class.

It was Mike's turn to laugh. "So, go ahead." The coolness he'd felt earlier had vanished. Instead, for the first time in quite a while, Mike felt full of life.

"What about public service? Aren't police officers supposed to do that kind of thing? Why not just consider this a matter of public courtesy? If you're in doubt, I could have my professor call you."

"Oh, Courtney—"

"I know, I know," she went on. "You're very busy. I understand that. But surely sometime in the next three months you could give me a couple of hours." She paused, but only for a second. "I wouldn't even ask you to get together with me in advance to go over any of the specific questions the class would want to ask." She rustled a handful of papers near the receiver. "I'd just let you go in there and talk about anything you wanted to talk about."

"You have questions? You already have a list of questions?"

"Yes." She rustled the papers in her hand again. "A lot."

"That many, huh?"

"That many."

"Well," he said hesitantly. "It sounds as if you've got me over a barrel. I'd be a cad if I said no after you've gone to that much trouble, wouldn't I?"

"Oh, I wouldn't be so hard on myself, if I were you."

He found himself laughing again. "Tell me, Courtney Evans, do you always get your way this easily?"

"The truth?"

"The truth."

"Actually, you're a tough case compared to most of them. It's probably the journalist in me. We're accustomed to being turned down, but we never take no for an answer."

"I'm sure nobody, but nobody, can resist you for long."

To her dismay, Courtney realized she was actually enjoying this mild flirtation. "I really don't think I should answer that. If I say yes, you're right, then you'll think I'm an egomaniac. If I say no, you'll be sorry you agreed to say yes, and then you'll try to back out of it."

"Your logic escapes me."

"Don't worry," she told him, trying to suppress a giggle. "It escapes me most of the time too."

Again he started to laugh. His chest expanded, and he felt a pleasant warmth spreading through him.

"Now about that list of questions, when would you like to meet to go over them?" he asked.

For an instant, she considered telling him they really didn't have to meet. Then she remembered Professor Conroy's no-nonsense expression. "Soon," she said, her answer swift and sure this time.

After they'd established a time, Mike said good-bye to Courtney and hello to the guilt caused by having said yes. He'd given himself a stack of reasons for not calling her, not seeing her again, but within a matter of minutes he'd melted like hot butter, giving her even more than she'd asked him for.

He walked to the sofa and straightened a throw pillow. One of the colors in the patterned weave of the pillow, a pale, pale blue, reminded him of her eyes. Her eyes were such a contrast to the darkness of her hair as it swept across her shoulders, he thought.

She was a lovely woman. There was nothing harsh-looking about her, nothing to find fault with. Her cheeks were rosy, and she had a way of holding her shoulders back that made her seem taller than her five feet three inches, and her walk somehow accentuated the sleekness of her petite figure.

He shook his head. There was nothing about her that he could find fault with. He even found himself admiring the way she'd cajoled him into doing exactly what she wanted. She'd almost made him believe he wanted to go along with her, despite his initial resistance. It was a credit to her skills, particularly when he thought about how hard-headed he usually was nowadays.

But a warning sounded in his head, loud and clear. He had no time for anyone else right now. He had enough problems at the moment. Leaving his profession would not be easy. Neither would the adjustment to civilian life, if he decided to do that, despite his friends' predictions of success and reasonable hours. Mike promised himself his interest in Courtney Evans would remain casual, no matter how beguiling she might seem.

He had always been a very private person, made so by a childhood spent in more foster homes than he cared to count. Now, with a failed marriage behind him, he intended to have only friendships in his life, nothing heavy or emotional.

Courtney waited until morning to return her mother's call. Mrs. Evans had called and talked to Courtney's answering machine while Courtney had been at law school. Somehow her mother could never keep track of her daughter's schedule, and nine out of ten times she called, Courtney was out. Her mother would spend a good minute-and-a-half haranguing the answering machine and Courtney's bad manners in using the contraption. Then, with a laugh, she'd hang up.

"Hi, Mom," Courtney said when her mother answered the phone in Austin.

"Hi, yourself. How are you?"

"I'm fine. How's Dad?"

"He's great. Out jogging already."

"What's up?" Courtney asked. "I know you've got something on your mind. I can tell by your voice." All her life she'd been encouraged to meet life head-on. It was a lesson she'd taken to heart.

"Oh, you always were a mind reader, honey."

"Sensitive, Mom. Call it sensitive. It sounds better that way."

"Okay, sensitive." There was a pause. "It's your sister Chris."

"Shouldn't even have bothered to ask, should I?" There was sadness in her voice. The Evans family was a large and close one. Courtney loved her parents dearly as well as her two older sisters and brothers. But her eldest sister, Chris, was constantly creating heartaches for all of them.

"She called me yesterday. Said there'd been a change in plans and she wouldn't be bringing Tracy for a visit after all."

Tracy was Chris's daughter from her first marriage. Courtney, along with everyone else in the family, had tried her best to get to know the child, but it had been hard, considering Chris's eternal quest for new marriages and her infrequent visits with the family. Chris had had problems ever since her first disastrous marriage to John Blume, and the family had suffered through them with her.

"Oh, that's too bad, Mom. I know how much you were counting on it."

"Something strange is going on. I just know it. Chris sounded bad."

In her mother's voice, Courtney heard a lifetime of disappointment. Alma Evans kept hoping for a miracle. She wanted Chris to come home and bring her daughter with her, but Chris had all but estranged herself from her family and spent most of her time trying to find a man to make up for her first husband's cruelty.

"I wish I could tell you not to worry about her, but I know it's useless, Mom."

"Oh, it's just that we've hardly ever had a chance to spend time with Tracy, and now that she's a teenager I'm afraid she'll be lost to us for good. That poor child can't be happy. She's never known any stability in her life."

There was nothing Courtney could say to dispel her mother's anxiety. To tell her her concern was unwarranted would be a lie. To tell her things would change with Chris would be another.

"I know, Mom, but there isn't anything we can do except let Chris know that we love her and that the door is always open. Things will work out eventually. I'm sure they will," Courtney said sincerely. When her mother didn't answer she went on, hoping to change the subject. "I had an interesting experience the other night."

"Oh?"

Describing what had happened to her, Courtney downplayed the threat to her life and made light of the episode.

When she was finished, her mother exploded. "Courtney, why didn't you call us? The very idea... Oh, I would have been so upset. I am now."

"That's why I didn't call. You would have been worried about me, and for no reason. Everything turned out fine."

"So tell me about the man who talked the criminal into letting you go. What was he like?"

"Professional," Courtney said cautiously. "He even made a follow-up visit."

"He came to see you?" There was a change in her mother's voice. Concern registered again.

"Yes."

"Did you talk to him?"

"I had to, Mother. He practically let himself in."

"Well, I'm grateful to the police for saving your life. But our family wants nothing to do with any of them. Do we?"

Courtney imagined Mike Harris's face, his patrician nose and chiseled jaw.

"No," she said quietly. "We don't."

"Not after what John did to Chris—"

"I know, Mom." Courtney had heard all of this a million times. She wasn't in the mood to hear it again.

For an instant she toyed with the thought of trying to explain to her mother that she was going to see Mike Harris again and why, but she quickly realized that was a very bad idea. Her mother would never understand how she'd gotten herself into all of this.

"How's the work going on the series?"

Courtney thought of Mike again. "Fine. No problem."

"That's my girl. You can handle anything."

I wonder what you'd say if you could see the mess I've gotten myself into, Courtney thought before saying goodbye to her mother.

Mike's day was going from bad to worse. When he awoke he had a terrible sinus headache, made worse by the heavy humidity in the October air. Then, when he arrived at the police department intent upon completing his paperwork, he was placed on immediate red alert. A family disturbance had been reported on the east side of town. Two policemen had been dispatched, but had returned to report that the wife would not file charges against her husband for assault. By the time they arrived, the man had passed out on the living-room sofa. The policemen thought the place should be watched closely for future problems and that Mike might be needed. His headache intensified.

Somehow Mike managed to make it through most of the day without any major disasters except that his headache didn't budge, despite his taking six aspirins in the space of three hours.

Forty-five minutes before his shift was scheduled to end, Mike received an emergency call. The man who had been creating a family disturbance earlier in the morning was at it again. Only this time he had crawled out on the fifth-floor ledge of his apartment building, threatening to jump. And he'd taken his eighteen-month-old baby with him.

As he rushed to the scene, Mike's headache threatened to become a full-scale migraine. He prayed he'd arrive in time, and then prayed that he'd be able to do some good once he got there. If only the man wasn't too drunk, or drugged, or crazed, he might be able to talk him down.

Mike's car screeched to a halt, and he raced into a run-down building. After sprinting up five flights of stairs, he arrived at the appropriate apartment.

Carefully, soothingly, he talked to the man poised on the ledge and finally climbed out beside him. His heart pounding, Mike tried to reason with the potential suicide for what seemed like hours. Finally the man burst into tears, handed Mike the crying baby, and crawled back inside.

"Take good care of her," Mike said a few minutes later to the paramedics who'd been waiting. He handed the infant to the nearest paramedic, relieved that no real harm had come to the poor child. He took one backward glance at the deranged man, who was being handcuffed, and headed to his car.

A job well done, he knew, but the price—the price was tremendous. Mike shook his head and walked to the police car. It wasn't until he was officially off duty and headed home that he remembered he had a meeting scheduled with Courtney Evans, and that he was already half an hour late.

He considered canceling. He was exhausted and wanted nothing more than to go to bed. But it was too late to call, so he hurried home, took a quick shower, gulped down three more aspirins and headed for Courtney's apartment.

"Hi," she said when he finally arrived.

"I'm sorry. I was detained—"

"Don't apologize." She wanted to tell him that she could have predicted he'd be late. Chris's husband had hardly ever come home when he'd said he would.

But right now she was too flustered to worry about anyone but herself. She had taken a deep breath when she'd first seen him at the door. A weak "hi" was all she could manage.

The man was mesmerizing, and she'd spent days and nights trying to conceal the fact from herself.

Besides his arresting dark eyes, which always seemed to be focused on her, and his smoothly chiseled features, he possessed a sensuality that was all too disturbing.

He was overwhelmingly male, and his presence made her feel totally female. No man had ever affected her this way before. It was almost more than she could handle.

Mike smiled warmly. It was the first time he'd been greeted cordially when he was an hour and fifteen minutes late.

He thought of his ex-wife, Nancy. She would have harangued him for hours for his lateness, demanded to know what his excuse was and then berated him anyway.

"Am I still welcome?" he asked.

"Are you ready to answer a few questions?" Courtney asked, her voice still weak. She opened her door wider. "If you are, come in," she said.

Tonight she wore her hair pulled back into a sleek chignon. She was wearing a crisp pink linen jumpsuit and a pair of heels. He found her amazingly attractive, and she looked more sophisticated than she had when he'd first seen her.

He stepped inside, catching the scent of her perfume as he passed her. "You smell good."

"Thanks." She closed the door behind him.

That remark was just the sort of thing she hadn't anticipated, and it made her a little nervous. He probably figured she had invited him over for something more than a mere interview. A man as all-out appealing as Mike Harris probably had plenty of women after him, Courtney thought. It irritated her to realize he probably thought she was out to seduce him.

But she wanted her professor to be happy, and she wanted her interview. Her reporter's stubbornness would see her through. "Let me fix you a drink."

"You won't get any protest from me." He sat down on one of the cushioned rattan chairs next to the sofa. He settled his head back for a moment, relaxing in the soft, comfortable chair.

"What'll you have?"

"Vodka on the rocks."

"Oh, a real drink," she said jokingly.

"I need it."

When she'd made his drink and a spritzer for herself she came back into the living room. "I'm so glad you could come," she said, handing him his glass. "I've been wanting to talk."

"I'm all talked out," he replied, more gruffly than he had intended, as Courtney sat down across from him.

There was no politeness left in him. He didn't want to talk. She didn't deserve his coolness, he knew, but he couldn't call up any semblance of good manners right now. He was too exhausted.

"Must have been a rough day," she said, realizing that Mike looked tired and slightly pale.

"I'm sorry. I'm not good company tonight."

"Don't apologize so much," she told him with a grin.

"It goes with the territory."

"I have a suggestion." Courtney stood up. "Why don't you finish your drink, put your head back and relax. I'll turn on some nice music and go into the kitchen and fix us a quick bite to eat. Then we'll do the interview."

Mike looked up at her. He could hardly believe she was for real.

After months of sleepless nights, loss of appetite and a general dissatisfaction with his life, Courtney was like a dream come true.

"I should go home and go to bed. I'm not much company."

"That doesn't matter. I can see that you're tired. I don't care about your role as companion nearly as much as I need to get this interview started. I'm selfish, Officer Harris. I'm thinking I might use your interview in my initial article. It's due in a few weeks."

Once she'd made her declaration, she smiled at him, her pale blue eyes lighting up as she did. He smiled back.

"A bribe," he said, eyeing the sofa longingly. "You're trying to bribe me."

"And it's a cheap bribe at that, chicken and rice with a few mushrooms tossed in for good measure."

"Consider me bribed."

She left him alone with his drink and his music. After a few minutes he found himself on the verge of sleep. Yet he wasn't too tired to remind himself that she'd made it plain why she had invited him to stay: he had something she wanted.

While she cooked, Courtney kept remembering how steady and calm Mike's voice had been the night he'd saved her from her attacker. The thought struck her that she was catching a glimpse of just how much that calm in the face of peril cost him. She went quietly about her cooking, listening every now and then for sounds from the living room.

She was more confused than she'd ever been. For years she'd had it drummed into her head that a man who wore a badge usually hid behind it, sometimes using it as an excuse for brutality and rage. Chris's husband, John Blume, had taught the Evans family that lesson. Chris's entire adult life had been unhappy because of him.

And now here was Mike Harris, asleep on her living-room sofa, a policeman through and through, practically the enemy. So far he seemed very different from Chris's husband. But it would be impossible to tell what Mike was really like until it was too late, and Courtney was determined not to repeat her sister's experience in any way.

When everything was ready she went into the living room and found him stretched out on the sofa, his eyes closed, his glass empty in his hand. "Mike," she whispered, "I hate to wake you . . ."

"I'm not asleep," he said, slowly opening his eyes at the sound of her voice. "I was just resting my eyes." He sat up.

"Dinner's ready."

He lay there, watching her intently. He flexed his muscular arms after a moment and sat up. Courtney realized that the lines she'd noticed around his eyes and beside his lips were the marks of stress, not age. He had a look about him that was quite powerful, yet always guarded. She wondered how one would go about separating the man from the police negotiator. She wondered if it was even possible.

"All right." He reached out, took her hand in his, and let her lead him into the dining alcove.

When she felt the strength of his hand on hers, she wondered why she was behaving this way. Why was she so aroused by a man she wanted nothing from, a man she told herself she didn't want to get to know?

There was no way she could excuse all this as the actions of a good reporter bribing her way into an interview. The mere idea was ridiculous. Her fears were real.

As they ate they talked, and Courtney became aware that several times Mike seemed to be on the verge of saying something, but always held himself back. And despite his appeal, that reticence worried her. She couldn't help but feel uneasy about the way he seemed to keep such a tight lid on his feelings and his thoughts. The conversation was in no way intimate. Any time she attempted to talk about some aspect of his personal life, he always changed the subject.

That reticence bothered her tremendously. It reminded her of her sister's ex-husband, another handsome, very private policeman. Courtney had nothing but bad memories of that man. She had seen Chris's battered face too many times. And she knew all too well the life her sister now led trying to forget the humiliation she'd suffered.

Mike ate heartily, and at the end of the meal he said, "I've never tasted anything that hit the spot like your chicken and rice. It almost makes me glad I was too—hic—excuse me, too tired to go out—hic."

She tried not to laugh. "Thank you."

"You're—hic—welcome. Excuse me," he said, reddening slightly. He put his hand over his mouth. "I seem to have developed a case of the hiccups."

"I know a surefire cure," she said and grinned.

"What? Salt? A—hic—hard blow to the back? What?"

She asked mischievously, "Are you ready?"

He began to smile. "I don't—hic—know. Something in your voice says I'm not going to—hic—like this."

"But it'll cure your..." She didn't finish the sentence. Instead she reached for her water glass, and without so much as an "I'm sorry about this," threw what was left of her water directly into his face.

Then she started to laugh, and at the same time ran around the table with her napkin to begin wiping off the water.

"Wha—what did you do that for?" he demanded.

"Surprise." She answered him matter-of-factly. "It cures hiccups every time."

There hadn't been much water left in the glass, and so it didn't take long to clean it up. When she was finished, Courtney looked down at Mike.

"Are you mad?" She realized now that she'd been testing him, looking for signs of an uncontrollable temper. Chris's husband had had one. She'd wanted to check out Mike's, wanted to find out he was very different from John Blume.

"I'm not overjoyed," he replied.

"But you don't have the hiccups anymore, now do you?"

He sat perfectly still for a moment. Then he looked up at her. "No, I don't."

"Then you can't be mad. It's just that I've seen this cure work every time. It's practically guaranteed. I could patent it."

"There's one thing you could do to make sure I don't stay angry," he said, and there was a huskiness in his voice this time.

"What's that?" She felt a fluttering in her throat that hadn't been there a moment ago, and caution flooded her mind.

"Come here," he whispered. He reached out and pulled her gently toward him, settling her in his lap.

It happened so quickly that Courtney wasn't sure of anything except that the fluttering feeling that had started in her throat was now coursing through her entire body. She wanted to say something, felt she should bolt away, but instead she simply looked at him.

He had the most perceptive brown eyes she'd ever seen, and an inviting mouth, strong and perfectly molded. His arms slid over her shoulders and settled across her back, pulling her closer to him. There was authority in his movements, an authority that seemed to make resistance impossible.

"Courtney, thank you for stopping my hiccups." His voice was a sweet, seductive whisper.

"You're..." This time she did try to get away.

He stopped her words by kissing her tenderly, his hands holding her chin to prevent her from turning away. She closed her eyes, giving herself over to the sensations that were flowing through her body.

His kiss was as quick as it was tender, and when he pulled away she opened her eyes in surprise. She hadn't thought he'd stop. And then he cupped her chin more gently between his thumb and forefinger before kissing her again. This time the kiss was deeper, more exploratory than before, expert, convincing.

When he finally released her, they both took deep breaths, staring into one another's eyes. Then she saw that he was beginning to smile.

"We haven't gotten to those questions you needed me to look over, have we?" he asked, his fingers gently stroking her throat.

"No," she murmured.

"What about tomorrow night?"

"Tomorrow night would be good." She frowned and shook her head twice, then suddenly began to nod. She knew she shouldn't let him back in her home, knew she shouldn't have anything to do with him, but despite her better judgment Courtney heard herself say, "Yes, I think tomorrow night would be perfect."

Chapter Three

Mike had taken himself in hand when he'd left Courtney's apartment that night. All the way home he'd played the role of devil's advocate, arguing with himself.

You promised you wouldn't get anything started with this girl, he told himself.

"I know," he said aloud, frowning as he tried to decide how to handle this new situation. But then he smiled slightly, remembering the look on Courtney's face when she had thrown the water at him. If anyone else in the world had done that he would have been furious. But he couldn't be angry with Courtney. Something about her made him happy, no matter how strangely she acted. She was fun and understanding and damned attractive. Despite his vow not to become involved, he wanted to be with her, wanted to hold her in his arms.

I'm going to keep this loose and fun, he told himself and prayed he could manage it.

He pulled into his driveway and got out, not feeling at all certain that he had decided anything.

Mike spent the entire next day anticipating his evening with Courtney. He left work smiling and drove directly to her house. As he approached her door he realized he felt happier than he had in months.

She was radiant in a cream silk blouse and slacks, her cheeks glowing with rosy color. Although she seemed to be making a point of not looking directly at him, there was a constant glint of amusement in her face. She was like a breath of fresh air.

"Hi," she said cheerfully.

"Hi."

"You look much more rested this evening," she told him, leading him inside.

"No ledges to walk on today. No babies to rescue."

"What?" she said, confused.

"Nothing," he answered, deciding that he didn't want to talk about his work at all. He didn't want to spoil what promised to be a pleasant evening. "Just my end-of-the-day mumblings. You'll have to excuse me."

"How about a drink?"

"No, thanks. Tonight we'll do this thing right. I'll take you out for a drink and then dinner. Maybe we can go to a club afterward, if you'd like."

She hesitated. "That sounds great, Mike, but it's not necessary. All I want is an interview."

He watched her face, noticing that she still refused to look him in the eye. "That's all I'd planned on, too. I just thought you'd like to do it in a different atmosphere. All I'm offering is dinner. Don't tell me you're afraid of having dinner with me."

"Afraid? Of course not."

His eyes were on hers, and something began to stir inside Courtney when she recognized the intensity of his gaze. The look was long and penetrating.

He frowned. "Maybe I'll interview you instead. Maybe I'll even get you to explain why you act the way you do with me. One minute you're warm and friendly. The next you're cold as ice."

Her thoughts were going wild. The man didn't mess around, and he understood her too well. It was as if he could read her mind.

"I don't know what you're talking about."

He shrugged. "Have it your way. Do you want dinner or not?" His expression abruptly changed, and eyes lit up. "I'm going to dinner." He turned and started out of the apartment. "You can come with me or stay. The choice is yours, only you can't very well interview me if you're not with me, now can you?"

She went with him. As they drove, Courtney thought about how intrigued she was by the controlled, aloof man who sat beside her. He was unlike any of the other men she'd dated. She sensed that he was complex, complicated. Despite her misgivings, she found him immensely interesting. She was even intrigued by the reticence that sometimes invaded his air of command. After all, she had to push him into agreeing to speak to her law class.

Mike took her to a place where a band played in one big room and in another were private booths where patrons could dine in a quiet atmosphere. "I'll make certain you have a good meal first. We can decide about the dancing later."

"No dancing. Question-and-answer time." She wouldn't let him keep the upper hand long, she vowed.

"Have it your way," he said with another shrug. "It's your loss."

When they were drinking their coffee, after dining on rare Chateaubriand and crisp Caesar salads, he looked at her, his intensity never more apparent. "You know, you're a fascinating woman," he said finally.

He couldn't help remembering the night they had met, the softness of her shoulders when he'd pulled her to him, the stricken look he'd seen in her eyes, the fear in her voice. When he'd put his arm around her to walk her home, he'd found her clinging to him. She'd been a woman in desperate need of him. Now he realized that she wasn't nearly as fragile as she'd seemed that rainy night.

She took a sip of her coffee, careful to keep her eyes away from his. This man had a certain authority that was evident whenever he spoke. She found herself hanging on his every word.

He was charming, but Chris's husband had been too—when he had wanted to be, Courtney reminded herself.

"I can't be as fascinating as a man who does what you do for a living." Intent upon ignoring his statement, Courtney said nothing while a waiter refilled her coffee cup. "Call it curiosity, but I want to know, do you like living on the edge of danger?"

"I must."

His answer had come a little too quickly for her. She stared at him, trying to read his true meaning. At the same time, she wondered what his reaction would be if she told him that the series she was about to do would concern people's problems with the police.

Aware of her questioning look, he took a deep breath and shrugged his shoulders nonchalantly. "Have you ever gotten yourself into something that later on you looked back on and wondered why you'd done it?"

Courtney nodded, thinking of the headstrong attitude that was always getting her into trouble. "Yes. Many times."

"I think it's that way with a lot of policemen. Maybe we don't see all the possible ramifications until it's too late to back out. The edge of danger is a tough place to stay for long."

He sounded weary, and there was a sadness in his voice that touched Courtney's heart. She found herself feeling sorry for him, and yet she knew he'd hate it if she said anything about what she was truly feeling. He was obviously a man who stood on his own. And in many ways he seemed different from John Blume.

"Well," she said, dragging the word out. "What about the questions and answers?" She'd gone to a lot of trouble to get him to sit still for an interview; she wasn't going to lose the opportunity.

He smiled indulgently. Then his smile grew, changing into a grin that she found arresting and very different from his usual solemn look. "Let's go dance," he said, picking up the check. "Then we work."

When they walked into the disco a slow song was playing, and the strobe lights were like tiny mirrors overhead, casting a checked pattern on their faces. Without even looking for a table, he led her onto the dance floor.

Taking her in his arms, he felt her settle against him, her body soft and relaxed. He moved her slowly around the dance floor, enjoying her gracefulness and noticing that they danced together very well. He held her close and closed his eyes, while they dipped and swayed to the rhythm of the music.

When the song was finished, Courtney looked up at him. "Well, you didn't tell me you were such a terrific dancer. Fred Astaire has nothing on you."

"Stick around. I'm a man of many surprises," he said, and chuckled, looking into her eyes.

A gentle ripple of tension started at the bottom of her spine and spread upward. She felt it tingling all the way to the roots of her hair.

There was no ignoring the attraction she felt for this man. The next song was a slow one, and Courtney found herself in his arms again without even knowing how she got there. It seemed that he held her a little closer than before, and she enjoyed the closeness, wanted to press herself even more tightly against his body. She could brush her lips against his neck if she chose. She could allow her fingers to lace their way into his hair if she wanted. Her mind reeled with the possibilities she was considering. She closed her eyes, and let herself enjoy her fantasies.

Much later, after they'd danced and then sat at one of the empty tables, Courtney was feeling flushed and all too aware of Mike's presence. Somehow he was getting too close to her too soon, and she needed to put some distance between them. "Give me some idea of your typical day," she said, trying to appear the unemotional and impartial reporter.

The noise from the band was loud, but not too disruptive. He'd found a table for them in the back of the room where they wouldn't be disturbed. It was dark. Mike could see the lower part of Courtney's face, but her eyes were in the shadows.

For a moment she thought he wasn't going to answer. Then, after **a** long hesitation he said, "There is no typical day."

"Okay." She backed up and started again, realizing that the last thing Mike had on his mind was an interview. "Tell me about your day today. It started when?"

"Six o'clock."

"What? You got up at six?"

"Yes. I reported for work at eight."

"After a shower, breakfast?"

He glanced at her. "You want to know all of that?" When he saw her nod, he sighed and decided not to debate the importance of giving every detail of his life. "At six a.m. the alarm goes off. I have my coffee pretimed so that it's made when I wake up. I drink my first cup while I make my bed. Then I take a shower." He stopped.

"Go on."

"This is silly."

"No." She shook her head. "It's not. Don't you see? These details give me the flavor of your life."

"The flavor of my life?" He began to laugh.

"Seriously, please go on."

"Where was I?"

"Taking a shower."

He grinned again, and she was pleased to see that he was beginning to relax. A guarded interview always proved to be a failure when it was translated to paper.

"Do you wear pajamas when you sleep?"

He eyed her. "Is that information absolutely necessary?"

"You don't have to answer if you don't want to."

"I don't believe you'd want to print anything so personal in a family newspaper. That's tabloid stuff."

"Okay." She laughed. "We'll go on. After your shower—what next?"

"I cook breakfast." Before she could phrase her next question he answered it. "Breakfast varies. Pancakes and sausage, eggs, Canadian bacon, cereal and fresh fruit. That's a week's worth."

"Sounds gourmet to me."

"I'd be happy to demonstrate."

She drew in her breath. It came shallow and quick. She wasn't sure how to get the conversation back on track. Finally she pushed back her chair. "Maybe we should go now. It's late."

"Interview over?" His question was a challenge. He'd enjoyed putting her in an uncomfortable position. Turn-about was fair play, after all.

"You don't get off that easily," she answered quickly. "I'll ask you some more questions on the way home."

Grinning at the way she'd recovered, Mike led her out of the disco, feeling better than he'd felt in a very long time.

Within twenty minutes, they stood outside Courtney's door. "I'll call you," he said, taking her key and unlocking the door for her. When he gave the key back to her he held her hand in his.

"No," she blurted out, feeling more afraid of her own instincts than she was of Mike. "I'll call you. For my class, remember?"

"I hope I made up for being so boring the other evening."

Courtney thought of the way he'd danced, of the way she'd enjoyed talking the entire evening, finding all sorts of things to discuss. She wanted to bite her tongue, but the words tumbled out anyway. "I had a great time."

"That's good to hear," he murmured, his dark eyes focused on her lips.

Her heart began pounding, and she had to fight to keep from raising her hand to her mouth. His staring was making her uncomfortable.

Mike leaned forward, and Courtney's breath caught in her throat. When their lips touched, everything changed. She pulled back, as if she'd been burned. Her feelings were much like those of the night before, only infinitely more powerful. Courtney hungered for more.

They came together slowly, each anticipating what was in store. Their lips met and parted, their eyes remaining open as they studied one another. His hands slid around her shoulders and pulled her to him.

The next time their lips met, Courtney felt waves of heat rising from within her. His mouth settled on hers possessively, as if to say no more teasing, no more brief kisses.

Their mouths were joined in desperate demand, his tongue finding hers, their breath mingling, their bodies trembling. Courtney didn't hesitate to respond to his kiss or to the feel of his hand as it moved in a slow, erratic path from her shoulder down to the swell of her breast.

Her fingers were warm against the small of his back, and she felt a wave of pleasure surge through her. She was like a woman set afire, mindless of anything but her own physical needs and desires.

Struggling for control, Mike moved away, although he still held her tightly, unwilling to give her up completely. "I've got to go," he said. "I—I'll call you."

Disturbed to discover how easily she'd fallen into his arms, Courtney closed the door behind him. She was a woman who'd never been ruled by her physical desires. Far from it. But Mike Harris stirred something inside her, something she was no longer certain she could control.

If she was smart, she told herself, she'd get out of this now, while she still could. But there were too many things she needed from him. She couldn't walk away, not just yet.

Chapter Four

Later that week, when Mike stood before her law class, Courtney no longer cared that she'd had to twist his arm to get him to agree to appear. He was as controlled and confident as she'd known he would be, with only a trace of the bored resentful look she'd seen him assume from time to time. The group was mesmerized, including Professor Conroy, who asked more questions than the students. They couldn't get enough of Mike, and gathered around him for individual questions after class. Courtney couldn't help but notice that every girl in the room watched with varying degrees of envy when she walked out with him.

After that, she didn't think it necessary to conceal her admiration. He'd done a terrific job. "You were wonderful!" she exclaimed as they walked to his car.

"I wasn't wonderful. I was factual."

"You call it what you like. I call it wonderful."

"I talked about the sort of things law students are interested in. That's why you enjoyed it." He hurriedly opened the door on the passenger side and saw that she was comfortable before going round to his door.

When he had slid into the seat and was putting the key in the ignition, Courtney studied him. The gray at his temples stood out in sharp contrast to the darkness of the rest of his hair. His rugged face was filled with character, and seemed more handsome than ever.

"You're very knowledgeable," she said when he had turned to look at her.

"Thanks." He stared at her, making no effort to start the car.

"What's the matter?"

"There's something bothering me." Now he was looking into her eyes, a hard, calculating expression on his face.

"Oh?" she said simply. The way he was looking at her made her uncomfortable. "What's that?"

"After the class was over, one of the young women who came up to talk to me said I should be complimented on changing your attitude about cops."

Courtney inhaled deeply.

"What was that all about? Do you have an *attitude*?"

She didn't want to discuss it, but felt she had no choice. "I suppose I do."

"Mind telling me about it?"

"My oldest sister was married the first time around to a rookie cop. He was a bully who enjoyed the power of his badge more than he should have. He hurt my sister, physically and psychologically. As of today she's on husband number three, still trying to prove how lovable she is."

"And all cops are supposed to pay for the one bad one you've known?"

He sounded so calm and logical that Courtney began to feel guilty. She didn't reply.

"You ought to think about giving some of us a chance." Slowly he put his hand out to her, and after a moment had passed she took it.

"It affected my entire family deeply. We all feel the same way," she whispered.

"Maybe the entire family just needs to meet someone who's not like the fellow they knew."

"It's pretty deeply ingrained in all of us."

"It's possible for anyone to change."

"You don't know my family. We're all pretty hardheaded," she said wryly.

"Those are the best kind of people, the hard-headed ones. Once they're won over, they're loyal and steadfast."

Saying nothing, she smiled weakly.

"Give me a chance, Courtney."

"For what?"

It was his turn to be silent. Then he said, "To be a friend."

She felt him watching her. There was a sudden tension between them. The desire she felt for him was stronger than ever. Courtney no longer had a choice. If she lost him now, she didn't know what she'd do. She nodded. "All right. I'll try."

"Now that I've done what you asked me to do, what now?"

"What do you mean?"

"I mean, if I call you again, will you see me?"

"Do you really want to see me again?"

For a long moment he stared into her eyes, and she had the uncomfortable feeling that he had to weigh the question very carefully before he answered it. When he finally said yes, she felt as if she'd had to drag his answer from him.

She managed a smile, not understanding this man or anything about him, knowing only that she was drawn to him—maybe too much so.

Over the next week they saw one another every night. They went to dinner, they went dancing, and sometimes they just drove around, arguing about politics, revealing bits and pieces of their pasts, and having fun, almost always having fun.

He took her to the symphony, and she discovered the music was lovelier than she could ever have imagined.

She introduced him to the Spurs basketball games and loved the way he turned into an instant fan, rolling up his shirtsleeves, eating hot dogs and popcorn till he swore he was stuffed, and learning the cheers before he'd even heard them twice.

There were problems for Courtney, problems she tried to ignore but soon found she couldn't. The most immediate one was that whenever they were together, she felt as if he was holding back, keeping something to himself that she wished desperately he'd share with her.

He listened to her talk about her family, seemed interested, asked questions frequently. He listened to her discuss her past, the men, the friends, the growing up, all of it, and again he gave her the impression of being intrigued. But he didn't talk about himself much. He told her very little, volunteering only scant information from time to time.

But she was falling for him. Each meeting drew her closer. Each kiss increased her desire, leaving her weak, longing for more.

One Saturday night, after they'd been out to the Lone Star Cafe for another sampling of delicious chicken-fried steaks and homemade onion rings, it started to rain again. They'd laughed, convinced that together they had the power to create stormy weather.

They ran down the street together toward Courtney's apartment, soaked before they'd gone more than a block. Mike was running ahead, Courtney slightly behind but trying to keep up despite her high-heeled shoes and her straight linen skirt.

"Mike, look," she cried.

He turned back and saw her bent over. He ran to her side. "What is it?"

A thin, bedraggled kitten was hunched against the brick wall of Courtney's apartment building. "Poor thing."

"It looks like a drowned rat."

"Oh, Mike, this kitten's hungry." She scooped it up in her arms, oblivious now to the rain that was pelting down on them. "I'm taking it home."

He put his arm around her, urging her ahead. "Well, come on then, before we all drown."

When they arrived at her apartment, Courtney went to fix the kitten a bowl of milk. Then she went into the bathroom and came back with towels for all three of them.

She dried the kitten, ignoring its whining complaints about being pulled away from the milk. She thought about offering Mike a robe to wear while she dried his clothes, but when she looked up he was standing over her, his wet shirt in his hands.

"I'll just throw this in the dryer," he said.

"What about your pants?" The two of them looked down at his wet slacks.

"What about them?" he asked teasingly, and they both smiled.

"I can give you my robe."

"Your robe? It wouldn't fit."

"I could offer you a blanket," she said softly.

Tension filled the air. "Where would the blanket be? On your bed?"

His eyes held hers. He sighed, then gave her a taunting grin that made her laugh.

"No," she answered. "It's in the closet. First door to your right down the hallway."

"Are you sure there's not a blanket on your bed?"

"I'll be happy to dry your clothes for you. If you don't want to use my robe, the blanket in the closet is all I can offer right now."

He caught the last two words, and he grinned again. "Fair enough." He went in the direction she'd indicated.

A few minutes later he returned, his slacks in his hand, a quilt wrapped around his shoulders, his hair still slightly damp. Courtney thought she'd never seen him look so inviting.

She looked away abruptly, giving the kitten her full attention. "I need a blow dryer for her."

"Her?"

"Yes. While you were out of the room, we talked. She told me a little bit about herself. Said she'd just as soon stay here for a few days as roam the streets."

"Who wouldn't?" This time it seemed to Courtney his tone was deliberately suggestive.

She ignored him. "What about a cup of hot tea?"

Mike leaned against the doorframe, casually holding the blanket around his shoulders. "Hot tea sounds good."

He'd made up his mind the evening before, when he'd taken her into his arms and then reluctantly let go, that they had to talk. Tonight seemed like the right time. He'd tell her how he felt about relationships. He'd let her be the judge of what the two of them should do from this point on. Whatever he did, he had no intention of hurting either her or himself.

"Let's take it into the living room," she said when the water for the tea was good and hot.

He followed her in watching her closely. "Aren't you going to get out of your wet things?" he asked. She was as soaked as he had been.

She put the tea cups down on the coffee table, almost spilling both of them. "I—I suppose I'd better." She forced a smile. "I'll be right back."

"If you need help—"

"No, thanks." With a hasty glance in his direction, she hurried out of the room.

When she was in the bedroom, changing out of her wet clothes, she had a vivid mental picture of herself curled up in Mike's arms under the blanket on her bed. The image was startling in its clarity, stunning in its implication.

Too soon, Courtney. Too fast. He's not the man for you to get involved with. You already know he's too private a person, too moody, she warned herself.

She finished dressing as quickly as she could, and hurried back into the living room, carefully closing the bedroom door behind her.

"Well, would you like some more tea?" she asked.

"No. I just want you to sit down here next to me. Here's your tea." He held the cup up for her, motioning her down beside him on the sofa.

"Oh, the kitten," she cried, unable to control her nervousness. She jumped up and went to find it.

She felt as if something would happen soon, and she was very apprehensive.

For years she'd been warned about his kind. But Mike Harris was different from any man she'd ever met, Courtney was sure of it. Nevertheless, he was an enigma to her. She'd learned to care deeply for him in an amazingly short time, but still she knew so little about the man behind the badge, so little about the man she was beginning to love.

So what was the problem, she wondered when she'd found the kitten and had no choice but to go back to face Mike. The problem, she told herself, was that her heart was beating so hard she thought it might fly out of her chest. The problem was that she was filled with energy, and she was helpless to get it under control.

But the real problem was that he was all male—more sensual, more frankly masculine than any man she'd ever been near. The man was mysterious, intriguing, his every look blatantly provocative. He was intense and driving. But there was something just below the surface that always made her feel uneasy.

"Here she is." Courtney sat down again, making the kitten comfortable in her lap. She began stroking the soft fur, which was dry at last.

Mike reached out and took a strand of her wet hair between his fingers. Over and over he gently curled it around his index finger.

He moved closer to her. She felt her breath leave her body as his lips caressed the fleshy part of her earlobe. She felt herself surrendering to the onslaught of feelings.

Don't think about this. Above all, don't think, she ordered herself. Thinking would destroy the moment. Thinking would destroy the feeling.

The feeling was all-important. As his mouth began to move on hers, feeling took over and her brain shut down.

She tried to pull away, but his strong arms held her fast. Her heart was hammering so loudly she was certain he could feel it, probably even hear it. But so was his. The tension in his body was like an electrical charge. They were on a dangerous course, and she knew she had to back out now or be lost forever.

She felt her lips part beneath his. His tongue probed gently, seductively, coaxing her into giving him entrance. It was maddening, completely maddening.

Instead of hating it, she found herself caught up in a whirlwind of passion as his tongue delved into the warm interior of her mouth, exploring, swirling, reaching as far as he wanted it to reach.

His sensuous caresses tormented her until she was nearly wild with longing. She wanted him every bit as much as he obviously wanted her, but she knew she had to stop.

Weakly, she began to fight, first twisting her body away from his, then pushing against his chest. She had to call upon every ounce of strength she possessed in order to exert any influence upon him at all.

At first she pushed at him like a baby, but then her resistance became stronger, especially when she realized the ramifications of succumbing to Mike's advances now.

She couldn't. It didn't matter that she wanted to. She couldn't.

"Mike," she cried. "Please don't."

He didn't want to acknowledge her protests. He was lost in his own tempestuous feelings.

Yet he knew she was right. She was voicing what he knew he should be saying to himself. All but overcome with desire, he reluctantly pulled back from her.

He put his arm around her, leaned back against the sofa with his eyes closed, and let out a sigh of protest. Relieved, she rested her head against his arm. She felt like an animal that had made its escape but didn't know where to turn next for fear of falling back into the trap.

"Let's talk," he said, when the silence between them had become uncomfortable.

"Let's not." She was serious. The evening had been much too extraordinary to let conversation disturb its memories.

"I need to." His words were firm and sure.

"All right," Courtney agreed finally. "But do you really want to talk, or do you just want to listen as usual?"

"Is that what I've been doing?"

"You know you do that to me all the time, Mike."

Her accusation was unplanned, but now that it was out, she was almost relieved. She looked up at him, anxious to hear his response.

Mike had been looking out the living-room window, but now, turning so that he was facing her, he took a deep breath. Now was the time to say what he'd been thinking for several days.

"I've had a lot on my mind lately," he began. "I've had trouble with my job for the past few months. I don't think I can manage it anymore; I'm completely burned out."

She watched him, feeling a pang of sympathy. He seemed cautious, and his gaze never left hers.

"I've pretty well made up my mind I'm going to take a desk job, but I'm not feeling great about it." He sighed again. "The job I've been trying to do is too costly. Working with people who're desperate enough to end their lives or those of others has become unbearable. My adrenaline goes crazy when I'm trying to talk somebody down from a ledge or out of a barricaded house with guns going off and people dying all around me." This time he shook his head. "I'm exhausted."

"I never realized things had been so rough for you," she whispered. "It must be terrible," she said with a shake of her head.

"That's why I haven't been as much fun as I'd like, why I've been so ambivalent." He tried for a smile. "To tell the truth, that's why I didn't want to get mixed up with you in the first place. I wanted to call you back when we first met, but I didn't, because I didn't think I could handle a relationship right now, and I didn't want to involve you in all of this."

"I see," she answered, finally understanding his sometimes contradictory behavior. She stroked the cat, which had left them for a while, then returned. She wished she had the nerve to reach out for Mike's hand.

He moved his arm along the back of the sofa, letting his fingers come to rest on her shoulder. "I was married before, Courtney. My job probably cost me my wife and my daughter. There were other complications, though." He looked sad. "I was gone a lot when I should have been home. I've got friends on the force who all say the same thing. It doesn't work when things are tough at home *and* at work. I'm not ready for anything heavy right now."

He was telling her how things would have to be, yet in the back of his mind there remained a niggling question. Wasn't he into this thing pretty deeply already? Wasn't he on some level already committed to Courtney?

She said nothing, not wanting to interrupt him for fear he'd stop talking.

"I'm fond of you. I'd like for us to spend time together. I've had more fun in the last two weeks than I've had in a long time."

"I've had fun too," she replied. She could tell from the look in his eyes and his serious expression that he was a man unaccustomed to intimate talk. The lines bracketing his mouth were more pronounced than before. He was extremely uneasy.

"But I'm not looking for any deep ties," he added. "I like you, Courtney. I like you a great deal. But I'm not into permanent commitments."

She looked curious. "You mean— Exactly what do you mean?"

"I mean marriage. Things like that. I was married once, and it didn't work out. I don't want anything to do with being married again."

She grinned. In a quiet voice she said, "Marriage. Oh."

"What's wrong? You don't agree?"

Courtney smiled kindly. "Marriage wasn't on my mind, either," she answered. "We've only had two weeks' worth of dates."

"I know, I know, but I just thought I ought to be up-front with you, tell you how it is with me," he said, a little defensively.

"I appreciate that, Mike. I really do. And I'm not upset. Remember, I have a few misgivings myself."

"I know. That's why we should approach this thing with caution. I want us to be open with one another."

She smiled happily, feeling as though he'd spoken to her heart. "I do, too, Mike. Oh, I want that more than anything else. Openness. Honesty. The two of us able to discuss exactly how we feel."

"Yeah," he murmured, a little shaky even as he agreed. He wasn't at all comfortable with conversations like this one. He'd spent too much energy keeping his emotions bottled up inside. He used his emotions at work, and that was enough. But Courtney was important to him. He couldn't deny that.

"Not wanting to think about marriage doesn't mean I don't care for you, you know." His eyes searched for understanding in the pale blue depths of hers.

Slowly Courtney lifted her face toward his, seeking out the comfort of his lips. When she found them, she brushed her mouth against his. The kiss was warm, friendly, not intended to communicate anything but affection and understanding.

When his lips began to nibble a trail toward her ear, she began to speak. "I want you to know, Mike, I'm not a woman who needs permanency or a marriage license to certify what I feel. I'm a woman with a career, who's involved in her own life right now. I'm very independent, and I'm certainly not interested in establishing anything heavy."

He was kissing the curve of her cheekbone then, his hands trailing along the back of her neck with the lightest of touches. She closed her eyes and tried to continue.

"Mike, listen," she said, pulling away. "I've had a wonderful family life. I made a mistake, got tied up with a fellow who wouldn't talk to me, wouldn't communicate. I discovered then that there are many things more important than being married. Besides that, I've watched my sister play musical marriages." She shook her head. "I'm a strong woman and I'm able to stand on my own two feet. Don't worry about me. The last thing I want is to tie myself down. I don't need it."

He gazed into her eyes, unable to believe his luck. Was she actually saying that she treasured the same things he did?

"I like my independence. I think it would be best for us if we date without the intention of getting serious," she declared.

"Do you understand what I'm saying about not needing any more complications right now? I'm trying to make up my mind about this police business, and it's going to affect the rest of my life. I'm a dedicated cop. It's a difficult decision."

"Believe me, I understand completely," she told him, and she did.

"Well, I think it's great. Really great that we see eye-to-eye on this thing."

It was true. He did feel great. But he couldn't shake the idea that he'd ignored his emotions for too long. He wasn't completely sure that he knew what it was he did want. Because suddenly he was surprised to discover that he wanted to ask her to move in with him.

You'd better have your head examined, Harris.

He plunged in anyway, ignoring caution. "You'll probably think this weird, but I was thinking. Maybe we..."

The telephone rang, jarring them both from the spell they were under.

"What?" she asked.

"Answer the phone first. Then I'll tell you."

She got up and went over to the rattan chair next to the telephone table. She bent over to pick up the phone. "Hello," she said on the fifth ring.

He saw her eyes widen, then watched as she began smiling.

"Chris, is that you?"

She sat down, listening. He could tell from the way she huddled over the phone that the conversation was an important one, and so he made no movement, not wanting to distract her.

"Chris, are you all right? Tracy? Well, yeah, sure." She paused. "Why not Mother?" Her voice rose then. "No, I'd be glad to have her. Of course—you know I would. It'll be wonderful. I can't wait."

She looked over at Mike then. She wiped her face with her hand and brushed away a strand of hair that had fallen across her face.

He tried to figure out the gist of the conversation, but what he heard told him nothing, and Courtney's expression was unreadable. He studied her, wondering what he was doing here, why he was placing his emotions in such jeopardy. No matter how much he tried to kid himself or her, he felt much more than he had ever intended to feel for Courtney Evans.

She talked for a while longer. When she hung up, she stared at the phone, then turned to him. "It was my sister. She's sending her daughter Tracy to stay with me for a while."

There was a curious mix of happiness and confusion in her expression. Mike took the news hard. He wanted nothing to interfere with what they were building. Whatever came into their lives now would be an interference. He resented it.

"What were you going to say before?" she asked, coming back to sit beside him. "Tell me what it was, and then I'll tell you about Tracy and Chris."

He sat there, knowing it would do no good to bring up anything like the prospect of living together. "Nothing," he said sadly. "It was nothing."

Chapter Five

The next morning, Courtney was up at the crack of dawn, leaning against the doorway to the spare bedroom, a frown clouding her face. She had only a few hours to convert this twelve-by-twelve rectangle from a cluttered storage room to a bright, appealing room for a sixteen-year-old girl she knew about as well as she knew her hairdresser.

No, she thought, rubbing her forehead. That was all wrong. She knew her hairdresser better than that. She'd listened to the woman recite her life history one day while spending four hours getting one of those fashionable frizz perms.

Knowing she'd be unable to come to any intelligent decisions until she'd had a cup of coffee, Courtney slowly made her way into the kitchen, wondering if sixteen-year-old girls drank coffee in the morning. She made herself a cup of instant and drank it as fast as the heat of it would allow. Then she hastily made another. The first one had done nothing to uncloud her brain. The second did very little.

A teenage girl? Who did she know who knew what one did with a sixteen-year-old girl?

Pamela. Her friend's name popped into her head, and with it the distinct memory of the problems and annoyances Pamela had had with her own daughter. Courtney felt her stomach tighten with trepidation. She hoped Tracy wouldn't turn out to be that sort of girl.

Not wanting to scare herself any more than she already had, Courtney dialed Pamela's number, forgetting the early hour. "Pamela," she said when a sleepy voice answered. "It's Courtney. I have to talk to you. Could you come over?"

"Courtney?" Pamela sounded as though she were talking from the bottom of a deep well.

"Yes," Courtney answered, only then looking at the clock. "Oh, no," she muttered. "Six o'clock."

"Yes, my friend— Correction, my former friend. It is six o'clock on Sunday morning and you want me to come over."

"I'm sorry, Pamela, but it's important and I forgot what time it was."

"It had better be important," her friend grumbled, but Courtney could tell that she was becoming more civil by the second.

"I'm sorry, really. I've been up for so long I thought it was much later."

"What's the matter?"

"Well, I've got a little problem." Courtney rubbed her forehead again. "Actually, it's not exactly a problem. My sister called me late last night. She's sending her daughter to see me."

"Her daughter?"

"Tracy. She's sixteen. A lovely girl. I haven't seen her since she was—oh, thirteen, fourteen, something like that. I've talked to her on the phone. I call on her birthday and try to stay in touch with letters and the like, but she's not much on correspondence."

"Who? Your sister or your niece?"

"Both. I mean, neither."

"How long is she staying?"

"Chris didn't say." Courtney drained her second cup of coffee.

"That sounds ominous."

"Oh, I don't think she'll stay for too long. My gosh, she can't, Pamela. The girl can't miss that much school. Chris has had some sort of emergency come up. She's making a fast trip to Europe, and she can't leave Tracy alone. It won't be long.''

"Okay," Pamela answered.

"But you've got to help me."

"What's the first problem?"

"The bedroom. It looks like a storage shed for a disaster-relief agency. I don't even have a bedspread. I don't know what a sixteen-year-old's room should look like."

"What it should look like and what it actually does look like are two entirely different matters. If you were decorating it for my Julie, I'd say leave it exactly as it is. She's most comfortable with that kind of atmosphere. The worse, the better."

"Come on, Pamela. Your daughter is a neat girl."

"Only someone who's never seen her room could say that." Pamela laughed. "Don't worry, I've got an extra bedspread. It's not great; it's one we took out of Julie's room when she went punk and wanted something in fake leopardskin."

"Can you come over?"

"When is the girl coming?"

"This afternoon."

"This afternoon?" Pamela screeched. "Say, you don't have much time, do you? I tell you what. I'll be over there in about an hour. Julie will sleep all morning anyway. I'll leave her a note."

"Thanks, friend."

"You're welcome," Pamela said. Then she added, "Besides, with a teenager in the house, you'll need all the help you can get and then some."

Courtney hung up, relieved to know that she had someone to share this seemingly insurmountable chore with, but reminded by her friend's conversation of all the things she didn't know about teenagers. She shook her head, telling herself not to worry too much about that. She looked forward to Tracy's visit and hoped it would give the two of them a chance to really get to know one another.

And then there was Mike. Last night had been wonderful in some ways, less than satisfactory in others.

First off, he was simply too tempting a man. Somehow, every time she was near him, she forgot that anything else mattered or even existed.

When he'd opened up to her and told her about his problems with his work, she'd realized she'd never felt closer to him. The idea of finding someone who wanted the same sort of sharing as she did meant more to her than words could express.

But would he really be able to share? Before last night, he'd never given her any indication that he could be anything like the sort of man he said now he wanted to be. And even in the middle of their discussion, she had felt him holding back, not really telling her as much as she wanted to hear.

His concern about not wanting problems in a relationship didn't really make sense. Every relationship had problems of some kind. That was life; it couldn't be avoided.

And was it human nature, she wondered, that made her care about a man whom she still didn't feel comfortable telling her mother about? It would be a long time before she stopped looking for signs that might in some way remind her of Chris's ex-husband.

For her part, that was why seeing Mike was so difficult for her. She felt handicapped, unable to be herself. For years she'd thought of men like him as being off-limits. But the man she was coming to know didn't fit the mold. He refused to be anything but himself. No matter how hard she watched or how long she waited, he refused to act like the stereotypical cop.

If truthful discussion was something he really was interested in, she vowed she'd broach the subject with him again as soon as possible, tell him what she was thinking and how she was feeling. She wondered what his reaction would be.

Courtney cooked herself an omelet and ate it standing next to the kitchen counter where she was making a list of things she had to do before Tracy's arrival. Mike and the problems surrounding a relationship with him deserved a special time, a time for concentrated thinking.

That didn't stop her from thinking about him, however. About his eyes when they met hers, about his hands, about the fire he was able to ignite in her with the slightest touch of his lips.

She told herself that the only way to accomplish anything was to stay busy, and after she cleaned up her dishes, Courtney threw on a pair of jeans, old tennis shoes and a paint-splattered long-sleeved knit top.

Knowing Pamela was coming to help made things seem less overwhelming than before. Courtney went into the guest room and began throwing out whatever she could. By the time her friend arrived she had whittled the mess down to only the things she was sure she couldn't live without.

"Hi. Thanks for coming." Courtney opened the apartment door for her friend, accepting a quick kiss on the cheek as Pamela, loaded down with all sorts of interesting things, entered like a whirlwind. "I don't know where you get your energy," Courtney commented, admiring the way her friend was always able to work one more task or one more activity into her busy day.

"My mother always said I'd get fat like the rest of the family if I didn't stay active. Every time I think of her and my four chubby aunts I turn into a regular dynamo."

"You are that," Courtney agreed, taking the bedspread and one of the two boxes she'd brought along with her out of her friend's hands. "An attractive dynamo."

Pamela spent hours pampering herself both mentally and physically. Her svelte figure and her perfectly coiffed and streaked blond hair were evidence enough of that.

"Discards from Julie's last room-remodelling job. There might be something here we'll want to use."

"I've cleaned out a lot of things."

"I saw the boxes out in the hallway," Pamela said, daintily making her way around the things she'd brought. She was heading for the guest room. "You're right. This place is terrible. I had no idea what a pack rat you were, Courtney." She stopped. "What is that?"

"My kitten. I found it. I've decided to name her Emily." She picked up the kitten which had just awakened and was stretching elegantly, ignoring the two women.

"You and your rescue missions, I swear." Pamela started picking through Courtney's box of old newspapers, tossing them into the air behind her.

"It actually looks better than it did."

Pamela cast her a pained look. "Are you bragging?"

Courtney began to laugh. "No," she admitted.

"Good." Pamela pushed up the sleeves of her sweatshirt. "Let's get this place fixed up."

It took them the rest of the morning to make things presentable, but when they were finished, Courtney looked around the room with pride. It didn't look half bad.

Along one wall, they had arranged the twin bed. Julie's discarded pink ruffled bedspread was pressed and neatly arranged with two small lace throw pillows decorating it. Across the room they'd placed an antique pine dresser, and beside it a rocking chair with a cane seat that had belonged to Courtney's mother. Courtney hoped Tracy would appreciate that homey touch. The white Cape Cod curtains they'd left as they were, dusting them after they'd washed the window. Tracy would have a view of the river, anyway, a view Courtney had always enjoyed. They'd hung two of Julie's pictures on the wall. They were of enormous blue-eyed white Persian cats, and Courtney thought they more or less tied the room together.

After Pamela left, Courtney spent an hour working on the outline of her first article. She had decided to focus it on Mike. She was sure most people would be fascinated by his work.

Her first article was due on Thursday. That gave her four days to finish it, but she'd found the article more difficult to begin than she'd anticipated. Mike Harris couldn't be encapsulated in a few terse paragraphs.

She looked down at the scattered mess of papers on her desk. There wasn't going to be enough time, not with a niece coming to visit her.

Impulsively she went to the telephone and called her boss. "Mr. Wagner," she said when he answered his phone. "I'm sorry to bother you at home on Sunday, but I need an extension on my series. I'm afraid I won't be able to finish the first article by Thursday as planned."

"Sorry, kid," he said with an indifference she knew too well. "I can't give you an extension. You'll just have to burn the midnight oil. I've got everything set up for Thursday, and it's too much trouble to change."

"Yes, sir," she said, "but something's come up."

"Courtney, unless it's death, in which case I won't be seeing you on Thursday and you won't have to suffer my wrath, just have that first article on my desk by eight o'clock that morning." He paused. "Come to think of it, have it on my desk late Wednesday so I can go over it." His voice lost some of its harshness. "Goodbye, Courtney. My lunch is getting cold."

Burn the midnight oil is right, she thought as she showered and dressed, slipping on a brown wool skirt and gold silk blouse for her trip to the airport to pick up Tracy. She'd just have to find a way to balance everything that was going on in her life so that she could get the article written.

The telephone rang as she was about to walk out the door. She caught it on the fourth ring.

"Hello there. I was hoping to catch you before you left." Mike's voice was full of good cheer.

For an instant, she tried to resist the warm feelings flowing through her. She tried to focus on something else, but nothing seemed as important as the spark his voice touched within her.

"I was almost out the door."

"Early, huh?"

"Nerves, I suppose. I'm anxious to see her. It's been a long time."

"I've been thinking about last night," he said, keeping his voice low.

"Are you at work?" She could hear conversation, and telephones ringing, in the background.

"Yes."

That explained his low voice. "I've been thinking about last night too."

"As soon as we can, maybe tonight, we need to pick up on our conversation. Some things were left dangling."

She wanted to ask what things he had in mind, but figured that, like her, Mike had probably mulled things over and realized that each of them could list enough reservations about their relationship to fill a thick steno pad. But reservations or not, her pulse had raced when she'd recognized his voice on the phone. And she couldn't deny how much she'd wanted to give in to his caresses the night before.

"Well," she said, a little breathlessly, "I don't know when we'll have time." She hesitated before going on. "I suppose everything's happening a little fast for me, what with my sister's call and all." In truth, she was still caught up in thinking about his kisses the night before. She didn't know what was happening to her.

"How long do you think your niece will be staying?"

"I have no idea."

"Our timing needs a little work. First we attract rainstorms whenever we're together, now this."

"A complication," she murmured, thinking of what he'd said the night before. He had told her he didn't want any complications, and he probably perceived her niece as one.

For a few seconds, Mike didn't even respond, but then he warmly wished her luck and said his good-byes, leaving her with the promise that he'd call later.

When she hung up, she was more confused about him than ever. He obviously thought Tracy's coming would interfere with their developing relationship, yet he'd kept his silence. If they were going to be open with one another, Tracy should probably be the subject of their first discussion.

Thinking about the effect Tracy's coming would have on everyone, Courtney realized that she hadn't yet called the one person who'd be most thrilled to know that Tracy was on her way.

As quickly as she could, Courtney placed a call to her mother, explaining what little she knew. Just as she'd thought, her mother was ecstatic. Alma Evans had always wanted to spend time with her grand-daughter. She repeated this to Courtney several times.

Hearing a slight note of sadness in her mother's voice, Courtney realized it was because Chris had bypassed her in favor of sending the girl to her sister.

"Mom," Courtney said, hoping to avoid any problems, "Chris thought it would be a treat for Tracy. She said Tracy's thinking about going into pre-law when she goes to college, and Chris thought she might like to visit me, to talk about law school and all. That's why she's sending her to me."

"I understand, dear," her mother replied in a quiet voice.

Courtney didn't know what else to say. She'd done the best she could. She told her mother she had to go to the airport, hung up and rushed to her car.

At the airport, Courtney checked the flight number at least a dozen times. She'd had Chris repeat it, so she knew it was correct, and she'd memorized it after she'd written it down, but she was still tense with worry.

What if the girl had somehow missed the plane and hadn't been able to get hold of Courtney? What if she didn't recognize Tracy? It had been a long time. Children changed a lot, especially during their adolescent years.

Courtney began walking toward one of the television monitors that displayed the schedule of arriving and departing flights. When she saw that Tracy's flight was due to arrive after a ten-minute delay, it did her nerves little good. She wanted to rant and rave at one of the ground attendants about the lack of precision that characterized airlines nowadays.

But she held her tongue, mindful that she was tense only because she had allowed a thousand little worries to creep into her mind. She began to pace, her eyes moving restlessly from her watch to the terminal area where the plane should park, and back again.

With time dragging, she wished she had thought of asking Pamela, or even Mike, to accompany her to the airport. She went over to one of the rows of plastic chairs, sat down in one of the cleaner-looking ones, picked up an abandoned newspaper and began reading it.

After a few minutes, Courtney slowly folded the paper up again, arranging it so that the front page was still in the front, then put it down where she'd found it. It was almost time for the plane to arrive, and she went to find the appropriate gate.

Minutes later, Courtney was nervously scanning the faces of the passengers as they came down the passageway. The plane had been crowded, and she had to look quickly through the crowd.

When it seemed as if most of the passengers had disembarked and she still had not found her niece, Courtney began to worry. She looked around nervously, wondering if she could have made a mistake.

When the flight attendants and the pilots began walking toward her, she began to panic. Where was Tracy?

"Excuse me," she said to a flight attendant who approached. "Are any of the passengers still on the plane?"

The pretty girl gave her a patronizing look. "No. Everyone has already deplaned."

"Thanks." Courtney whirled around and ran to the ticket counter. "Excuse me," she said. "I'm looking for a passenger. Tracy Blume. Was she on the roster for Flight 474?"

The woman looked as though she needed a coffee break. With an air of indifference, she began scanning the rosters. "Flight 474?"

"Yes."

"Tracy who?"

"Tracy Blume." Courtney didn't know why she had the urge to keep talking. She hated the way her voice was getting higher and higher, faster and faster, with each passing moment. "Tracy came from Dallas. She was supposed to be on that plane. Her mother gave me this flight number on the telephone yesterday."

"Tracy Blume." The woman took a pencil out of her hair and tapped the counter impatiently. "A no-show."

"A no-show," Courtney repeated.

"No-show. Luggage was tagged and sent through."

"Luggage?" Courtney repeated weakly.

"Yeah. You know, the stuff that you put your clothes into and send along with you when you go on a trip. Luggage."

Courtney ignored the woman's sarcastic comment. She was too worried to care what anyone said.

"When's the next plane due in from Dallas?"

"Forty-five minutes. Flight 479. Same terminal."

"Thanks," Courtney said as she spun away. Running to the first telephone booth she saw, she dialed Chris's number in Dallas.

"Please be there. Don't have left yet," she pleaded as one ring followed another. "Come on Chris, don't do this to me."

On the eleventh ring, she gave up and told herself to be calm. She went to the baggage area, where two lone suitcases were traveling along the conveyor belt. When Courtney picked them up, she saw that each was clearly identified as belonging to Tracy Blume.

She had no trouble from anyone about taking them with her as she trudged back to the reception area to wait for the next plane.

On the off chance that her sister might have been out for only a few minutes, she stopped and dialed her number again; but again there was no answer. Then she sat and waited for the next plane from Dallas.

Three hours later, she'd talked to every official of the airline in San Antonio and Dallas, but she'd learned very little. One employee in Dallas remembered tagging the girl's luggage, checking her ticket and giving her the estimated boarding time. That was the last time anyone remembered seeing her.

Courtney drove home, despondent. What was she going to do?

When she reached her apartment, she carried the suitcases inside and put them down in the room she'd been so busy preparing for her niece only hours earlier. She looked around the room, then went into the bathroom, fighting off the nausea that had been her constant companion since she'd found out Tracy was missing.

She put a cold compress on her forehead and stared at her reflection in the mirror. What could she do? she asked herself for the hundredth time.

On the way home, she'd thought of calling Mike. He'd know what to do immediately.

But less than twenty-four hours ago he'd said he wanted no complications. He didn't want to tackle any additional problems, regardless of whose they were. Hadn't he made that emphatically clear?

Did she dare ask him for help? Her panic and her fear told her that she would have to. But she didn't think it was a good idea. He'd been adamant about his own needs.

Anxiety had such a strong grip on her that she didn't register the sound when the phone rang the first time. By the second ring, though, she was barreling her way into the living room.

As she was running, so were her thoughts. She was convinced it would be her niece. Tracy would say she'd gone off with some friends and had been unable to reach her aunt. Her excuse would be typical for a teenager, illogical but forgivable. Courtney would be the perfect aunt; she'd forgive Tracy but give her a stern admonishment always to let her know where she'd be.

"Tracy?" Courtney said breathlessly.

"Courtney?" It was Mike.

"Yes," she said mournfully. "It's me."

"Our connection's bad. Your voice didn't sound like you."

After a moment, she said, "It's me, all right."

"Did everything go as scheduled? Did you pick up your niece?" He waited. "Courtney? Courtney, is that you?" he demanded when he heard her sobbing. He'd never heard her cry before. She sounded terrible, as if her heart was broken.

"Mike," she cried. "It's Tracy."

"Courtney, calm down and tell me all about it," he said gently.

"Tracy wasn't there," she sobbed, trying to get hold of herself, knowing she must be impossible to understand.

She desperately needed someone to tell her troubles to, someone who cared enough to help. She didn't know whether Mike really did or not, but she was beside herself with worry.

"Okay, Courtney. Sit down. Take it easy. I'll wait. You've got to be able to tell me what's happening, and I'm afraid I can't understand you if you keep crying like this."

She did as he asked, and didn't try to speak until she could control her sobs. It took her a long time.

"Mike, I went to the airport," she was finally able to explain. "And I waited, but Tracy didn't get off the plane. Her baggage was there, but she wasn't." She took a deep breath and held it, fighting back a sob that was lodged in her throat. "And then I waited for all the flights after that, but she never came. Mike, she's disappeared."

Unable to contain herself any longer, Courtney began to cry again. She had terrible visions of gruesome possibilities, the kind that filled the front pages of the newspapers and were flashed on the television screen nightly.

"Courtney, I'll be right there. Don't do anything except sit by the telephone. I'll be right there."

"No," she cried. "No. I don't want to involve you in this."

"What?"

"You heard me," she said.

"I *am* involved," he answered tersely, hanging up without another word.

"Thanks," she murmured to an empty line, feeling enormously relieved to know that he would be by her side, this policeman who'd rescued her once and might be able to do so again.

Yet she knew he didn't want to be involved in this, and that disturbed her more than she was ready to admit. Admitting it meant she'd have to find a way to deal with it.

Chapter Six

Before driving away from the police station, Mike took the time to rig the cherry dome light on the roof of his unmarked police car and turn it on. He wanted to get to Courtney's place in a hurry. If he was questioned by anyone as to whether he was on police business or not, he'd decided to say "yes."

He took the first corner on two wheels, cautioned himself about getting to her apartment in one piece, then slowed down slightly. He took the second corner on three wheels and slowed down a little bit more. His adrenaline flowing, Mike began to feel a throbbing in his head. His first headache of the week was well on its way.

With tires screeching, he pulled into an empty parking place in front of her apartment, jumped out of the car and raced up to her door. "Courtney," he said, knocking loudly.

When she answered the door, she looked the picture of dejection. Her soft black hair fell across her reddened eyes. Her cheeks were streaked with tears. She was the essence of misery, and he had a sudden temptation to take her into his arms and promise her that everything would be all right.

But years of experience had taught him that offering false hope never did any good. He merely took her to the couch and sat beside her. His hands came to cover hers, warming her fingers and sending a ripple of pleasure through him. Even through her sorrow he saw the flicker of surprise in her eyes.

Courtney had wanted to be strong when he saw her. Crying when she was on the telephone was one thing. She wasn't at all proud of herself for having done that, but falling apart when he came to her apartment was a different matter. She had wanted to be strong when he saw her. She didn't want to appear incapable of handling her own problems.

But the fear was too overwhelming, the tension too great. After a few moments she leaned against him, her head pressing on his collarbone.

He could smell her perfume, feel the warmth of her body. He held her tightly to him.

"Sh-she," Courtney began, her tears choking her.

"Don't try to talk. Just relax." He began to rock slowly back and forth with her, hoping to comfort her.

"I, uh…" She shook her head. "I don't know why I'm going to pieces like this," she said finally.

"Because you've been given a major responsibility and things got beyond your control before you even had a chance to take control. Because you're scared."

Hearing him give voice to her concern made her feel a little better, and feeling the comfort of his arms made things seem more bearable somehow.

She dried her eyes against his jacket, blinking at the unexpected roughness of his tweed sports coat.

"I'm all right now. I'm sorry to have involved you in this. I simply didn't know who else to turn to."

He could see the strength in her take hold. She sat up straighter and began to speak. He wanted to interrupt her, to tell her what he thought of her apology, but he decided to let her do the talking instead.

"As I told you over the phone, I went to pick her up, but she wasn't there. I spoke to the people in charge. They had her two suitcases. But she had never checked in with her ticket. Someone in Dallas says he remembers her. At first he said he'd thought he'd seen her leave the terminal. Then he changed his mind. He's not sure."

"Have you contacted your sister?"

"She's already on her way to Europe. Paris, I think."

"Do you know where you can reach her when she arrives?"

Courtney frowned. "Tracy was bringing Chris's itinerary with her." She bit back the tears.

"Have you spoken to your mother? Maybe Tracy changed her mind, went there instead." Methodically, as he had done on so many past occasions, he questioned her, following all the correct procedures.

"I doubt that Tracy even remembers where her grandmother lives. She hasn't visited any of us in a long time."

"Where are the suitcases?"

"In her—in the guest room."

"Let's call your sister's house again. Maybe the girl went back there."

"The girl's name is Tracy." Courtney's voice had an edge to it.

She was testing him; he knew it, and he was prepared.

Mike nodded, as if her remark and its coolness had been nothing out of the ordinary. "Yes," he said soothingly. "I know."

"I'm sorry," she began. "It's just that I hardly know this poor child. I don't even have a recent picture of her, and I feel so bad about all of this."

"I know." He took her hand again to comfort her. "I know how you must be feeling."

"Mike, if something's happened to her, I—" She couldn't finish the sentence.

"Hey, that kind of thinking won't do us any good. You have to help me now. Let's sort through this thing again and see if we can come up with anything." He had her repeat word for word what Chris had told her the evening before, interrupting her occasionally to write something in a little notebook he had retrieved from his coat pocket.

After a minute or so had gone by, and Courtney was calm once again, Mike said, "I need a little more information from you, and then I think we ought to have a look in those suitcases of hers. We might find out something from them."

"Oh," she cried, jumping up and rushing for the guest room. "Why didn't I think of that? Maybe Chris's itinerary is in there. Maybe there's a note of explanation." Then she stopped herself, coming to an abrupt halt in the doorway. "That's crazy, isn't it?" she asked, as if she'd just heard herself for the first time.

"It's not crazy at all," he replied.

Mike could have told her that what she was experiencing was common, nothing to be alarmed about. In times of great stress, people tended to grasp at straws.

"First I'm going to call this in to the police," he said.

"I thought you had to wait twenty-four hours."

He smiled. "I'll exercise one of the few privileges we policemen have."

"Can you give me any guess as to her current height or weight?"

Courtney tried to think. Her sister was five-foot-seven, and Tracy's father had been a good six feet tall. "Maybe five-foot-six or so. She wouldn't be completely grown yet, would she?"

Watching Mike nod his head in agreement, Courtney realized how little she knew about Tracy.

"Hair?" Mike asked, picking up the phone.

"Her hair is black, like mine, unless she's dyed it or something," she said, thinking aloud.

"Mother's full name?"

"Chris Evans Blume Martin Banks."

He gave her a quizzical look.

"Three husbands," she explained.

"Current husband?"

"Malcolm Banks. At least, I think they're still married. Don't ask me why, but something tells me this sudden European trip is more than likely part of an effort of Chris's to keep her third marriage from falling apart."

"Address?"

"They live in Highland Park. I'll have to find the address." She headed toward her bedroom. "Give me just a minute."

When she returned, address book in hand, he copied the information. "Why don't you sit down while I call this in?'' Aware of the paleness of her skin, he said, ''You look exhausted.''

She reluctantly did as she was told, but she was too nervous to be still. While he talked to someone at the police station, she paced the floor.

She'd cried enough, shed all the tears she could shed, but it hadn't helped. She had a vision of her niece, alone, frightened, waiting for her. But she couldn't let herself keep thinking that way. It did her no good. She had to block those visions out, she told herself, if she wanted to be able to think clearly.

When Mike finished talking to his office, he said to her, ''They'll put out a description on the wire. They'll check first with the authorities in Dallas, let them know what we're looking for.''

Wringing her hands, Courtney searched his face for some indication of what he was thinking. ''And? I mean, what do we do now?''

''Wait,'' he said.

She heard a hint of apology in his voice. ''Wait? You mean you want me to simply sit down here in this apartment and wait to hear from someone?''

He nodded his head.

''Well, I won't. I can't do that.''

''What is it you think you should be doing, Courtney?'' He slumped down on the sofa, running his hands through his hair.

''I don't know. Something. Anything. I've got to call my mother.''

He glanced up in time to see the pained expression that crossed her face when she mentioned her mother. "Why don't I make some coffee for us first? Calling your mother can wait a few minutes, don't you think?"

Slowly he got up from the sofa and went to her. He tried to take her in his arms to comfort her, but she took a reluctant step back.

"I should call her now."

"In a minute."

This time he obeyed his first instinct and, putting his arm around her, gently led her into the kitchen. He walked with her to the stove and smiled down at her. "Don't you have a coffeepot, or any real coffee?"

She smiled back, appreciating his kindness at such a difficult time. She realized he was trying very hard to keep her from falling apart completely. Confident that he knew what he was doing, she felt a wave of relief wash over her. Despite everything, she knew she was fortunate to have him at her side.

"Somewhere in the back of that cabinet right there," she said, pointing, "is the coffeepot. If we're lucky, there'll be a can of coffee in the freezer. I keep it for when my mother comes to visit me, which isn't too often."

"Why don't I look for the pot, and you see if you can find the coffee." He gently placed his hands on her shoulders and turned her toward the refrigerator. "I can't imagine a woman who likes instant coffee," he said teasingly as he rummaged through the cabinet.

"I don't drink much brewed coffee. Instant's fine for me."

"Here's the pot."

"Lucky you. Here's the coffee," she said, closing the freezer door. She tried to peer through the frosty plastic lid. "Let's hope there's enough in here to make a full pot."

Yes, he thought, we'll need a full pot. Keeping a vigil like the one he imagined they had ahead of them would require lots of strong coffee, and nerves to match.

"Here." He took the coffee from her. "Let me make this. I'm obviously more experienced at this sort of thing."

Handing everything over to him was easy, she thought as she watched him fill the pot with cold water and measure out the ground coffee. He seemed right at home, as if it were perfectly natural for him to be waiting on her.

Despite her problems, she was thinking about him. He had that attitude that she'd responded to in the beginning, that authoritative take-charge air. There were times when she resented it, even envied it, but this evening she found herself most appreciative of it.

"Why don't you go and sit down?" he urged her. "I'll bring the coffee in to you."

But she couldn't. She needed to be doing something—anything to take her mind off her worries. "No," she said quietly. "I've got to call my mother."

Convinced that it would do no good to argue, he let her walk away without protesting. Instead he began opening cabinets, searching for two mugs.

"Hello, Mom," she said when her mother answered. "It's Courtney." She hesitated. "Mother, I have some bad news."

With the mugs of hot coffee in his hands Mike entered the room. He could see the distress on Courtney's face and hear it in her voice. His heart went out to her.

Quickly she told her mother what had happened. And then Alma Evans started in with a hundred questions. "I don't know, Mother. I don't know," Courtney answered over and over again.

Seeing the frustration in her face, Mike took two long strides across the room, put the coffee down on the coffee table, and without giving her any warning took the receiver from Courtney's hand.

"Mrs. Evans, my name is Detective Harris. I'm with the San Antonio Police Department. I'm a friend of your daughter's."

Speechless with surprise, Courtney watched him take over. She listened apprehensively as he began to explain things to her mother. But soon her anxiety over his taking the telephone out of her hand waned. Calmly and confidently he was answering the questions put to him.

And, listening to his side of the conversation, Courtney was sure her mother was feeling better, too.

He motioned for Courtney to sit down, and he handed her the coffee while still keeping up his end of the phone conversation. He smiled at her, then winked when he said, "Yes, Mrs. Evans, I'll be happy to keep you informed." He turned toward the windows. "And Mrs. Evans, we're doing everything possible to find her." He waited. "Yes, I'll call you back at eight o'clock, if not before. Yes, you're welcome."

He hung up the phone. "Your mother sounded very nice." Picking up his coffee, he came to sit beside Courtney. "There, that wasn't so difficult, was it?"

"No. Especially with you running interference for me," she answered. "Thanks."

"No thanks necessary." He began to drink his coffee.

She watched him, thinking of how he'd told her he wanted no complications in his life. Why had he come to her aid now? Was it because he cared for her, or because he was a professional and was doing what any professional would do?

"When someone can handle my mother like that, I'd say thanks are very much in order."

"Especially a cop?" He watched her nod her head reluctantly. "She was fine."

"Exercising grace under pressure, you mean?"

"Yes." He looked at her and smiled. "Let's get some more coffee, then have a look at those suitcases of Tracy's."

"Yes," she said, wondering if he'd be this good with anyone he worked with. Was he treating her specially, or had she become just another police investigation to him?

He refilled their mugs and returned to the living room. "Okay," he said, handing her the correct mug, "let's go."

He took her arm and helped her up. When she felt the power in his grip and noticed the sure way he went about taking care of her and the matters at hand, she breathed a sigh of relief. No matter what his reasons were, she had to thank God he was here. She didn't know what she'd do without him.

"Here," he said quietly, "you sit on the bed, and I'll open the suitcases."

Mike put his mug on the edge of the round table by the bed, picked up the larger of the two expensive leather suitcases and, putting it on the bed, opened it easily. He turned it so that Courtney could get a better look at the contents.

"While you look through there, I'm going to call my office," he said, going to the living room.

Carefully, Courtney began to sort through Tracy's suitcase. The girl had packed all her bulkier items together: sweaters, jeans, boots, tennis shoes, a pair of black high heels and a thick fleece robe the color of cotton candy. Courtney looked through everything, but there was nothing that might give them any clue as to where the child could be.

Feeling Mike's presence, Courtney looked up to see him standing in the doorway. There was a look in his eyes that disturbed her. "Any word?" she asked, feeling her heart swell with concern.

"No." He shook his head. "Nothing from hospitals, highway patrol, or police."

She bit her bottom lip, her mind awash in possibilities.

"Hey, I said they'd had no report of her, Courtney. So far, so good."

She sighed and closed her eyes, feeling the need to block out everything around her.

And then Courtney felt the heat of his body as he sat down next to her, putting his hand on her shoulder. She blinked and looked up at him. She started to speak, but no words came as he tenderly brushed his lips across her cheek and then across her temple. His fingers moved up to rub her nape, softly at first, then with more firmness, finally massaging her too-tight muscles.

"Tilt your head forward," he said, turning her so that he could better reach her neck.

"Ahhh," she cried as her sore muscles responded to his ministrations. His touch sent shivers down her spine that had nothing to do with the tension of her neck. Her nerves were alive with stimulation.

"Maybe this will help." He ran the flat of his hand across her shoulders with a firm stroke. Then he kneaded her shoulders with a grip that was powerful and hard.

"Oh." She hated to complain, but it was rough.

Keeping up the pressure, he said, "You need it. Can't get the tension out without suffering a little first."

Finally she began to feel her body ease just a little, and her shoulders didn't feel quite as hard as before. He massaged her neck, until she began to relax against him.

Soon she felt as though she were drowning in the sensations created by his caresses. Suddenly the tension inside her was different from what it had been, seemingly centered deep within her. She thought about the taste of his lips, the security and warmth that the memory of his embrace evoked.

"Thanks," she said quietly, when after a little while he broke the spell by standing up and reaching for the second suitcase.

"You're welcome. You can reciprocate sometime."

"Mmm." She rubbed her neck with her hand, tracing the path he'd created, trying to close her mind to the spell he'd created with his touch.

"Are you through with this suitcase?"

"Yes," she said, wishing he were still caressing her.

He shut it quickly and put it down on the floor before retrieving the smaller one. "Let's see what's inside here."

He opened the suitcase and began searching it himself.

Mike saw something on top of the clothes and picked it up. "Maybe this will—"

"A book," she interrupted.

"It's a diary." He turned it over in his hand. "At least the cover says it's a diary." The book was sealed with a clasp that required a key.

Both of them rummaged through the suitcase for the key, but found nothing but underwear. Mike glanced at Courtney. "I'm going to break the lock."

She looked at him doubtfully, hating to do that to Tracy.

"It may be important," he added, waiting for her to give him the go-ahead.

"I know." She shrugged.

Without a second's hesitation, he popped it open and began to scan the pages. "Listen to this," he said when he'd read the last entry.

Courtney held her breath, feeling guilty and sad and confused all at the same time. "I'm listening," she said, gripping the side of the suitcase.

"My mom says I have to go to San Antonio while she chases after Malcolm. Who knows how long that could take? I don't want to go. I barely know Aunt Courtney, and Mom's sprung me on her practically without any warning."

Tears came unbidden to Courtney's eyes. "She sounds like a very sad girl."

"You're right." He was busy skimming through the book. "Look at this." He handed her the diary open at the front. Glued to the inside front cover was a picture of Tracy.

The girl in the picture stared back at Courtney with clear eyes that were bigger and bluer than Courtney's. She had a delightful smile on her lips, but somehow the smile didn't reach her eyes. The girl's shoulder-length hair was black and curled around her face in the latest style.

"She's beautiful," Courtney said with a sigh.

"She looks very much like you."

"Really? You really think so?" Courtney was flattered.

"Absolutely. You could pass for sisters."

Clutching the book to her breast, Courtney looked up at Mike. "We have to find her," she whispered. She opened the book again and gazed down at the picture, feeling the panic sweep over her again. "We must."

He gave her a moment to come to terms with her thoughts. Seeing the girl's face made the reality of her disappearance that much more difficult to deal with, he knew.

"What now?" she asked, still choked with emotion.

His dark eyes met hers, and he said, "My hunch is that I need to make a little trip to Dallas."

"Not alone you don't," she told him smoothly, as if she'd been waiting for just such a declaration.

"You have to stay here in case she tries to get in touch with you."

"Someone needs to, I agree," she said, "but it isn't going to be me. If you go to Dallas, I'm going with you. She's my niece and my responsibility. In fact, I can handle it alone if you'll tell me what to do. Whatever happens, I intend to find her."

He watched her face as she talked. There was no denying that the longer she argued, the more persuasive she seemed. And he thought he could see by the set of her shoulders and the tightening of her jaw that she was spurring herself into action. She felt she'd be of some help if she went, and she needed to be involved right now.

"Who'll watch your apartment, answer your telephone?" he asked, knowing she'd have some sort of answer.

"I have a friend, Mary Claire. She was once my closest friend. If I ask her, she'll apartment-sit for me, and when she's not here, she can switch my telephone to call-forwarding so that it rings at my mother's house in Austin. My mother would want to be a part of this too."

She was sounding like the old Courtney: sure of herself and her intentions.

He smiled. "Got it all figured out, huh?"

"Not at all. But I know that if you think Tracy's in Dallas, I want to go there."

He reached out and took her hand. Both of them stood. Mike swept her into his arms, feeling her resistance but determined to ignore it.

"Let me hold you, Courtney."

"You don't have to go to Dallas, you know. There's really no need. You can tell me what to do and I can take care of everything myself." She suspected that he was only helping her out of a sense of duty, and wanted to give him the opportunity to back out gracefully.

Aware of the fragile state she was in, he chose not to respond directly. "You're repeating yourself, and it's unnecessary. I heard you the first time."

He held her tightly, wanting to protect her from the emotional pain she was experiencing.

"Courtney?" His voice had somehow become a hoarse whisper.

He brought his hands up to cup her face, looked deeply into the blue depths of her eyes and knew the meaning of need. He wanted to protect her. Her palms came to rest lightly on his upper arms, and beneath his coat, his skin tingled in response.

He bent his head toward her. A soft, wispy breath misted his lips in the split second before he captured hers. Tenderness flooded his senses and coupled with the fierce desire he'd come to know too well.

His hands left her face to follow the contours of her throat, to slide across her shoulders. She did not resist, and he drew her even nearer.

His tongue curled around hers, sensuously. He intended, despite his own desires, to go no further than this kiss. He wouldn't take advantage of her vulnerability.

When he reluctantly took his mouth away from hers, he kissed her cheek and then her neck, rejoicing in the way she threaded her fingers through his hair. He hugged her to him then, taking comfort in the feel of her body against his, hoping he was giving her comfort also.

"You need to rest," he whispered. "I'll stay by the phone."

"What about Dallas?" His touch felt so soothing, so wonderful, that she was unwilling to let him go.

"Tomorrow. If we don't hear from her tonight, we go tomorrow."

Gently he picked her up and carried her to her room. Laying her down on her bed, he removed first her shoes, then loosened the buttons of her skirt. As he went about his ministrations, he deliberately kept his eyes away from hers and his touch as clinical as he could.

He knew that one look, one caress, would spell trouble. Right now, he wanted only to help her, protect her, care for her.

He wanted to lie down beside her and give her everything he could offer in the way of comfort, but he knew it wouldn't be right. She was defenseless tonight, and he had to protect her, even from himself.

He left her there and turned out the light, aware of the way her eyes followed his every move. It took all the control he could muster to force himself away from her.

She was a very special, very vulnerable woman. Suddenly Mike wondered if it was he who might prove vulnerable to her.

Chapter Seven

After waiting overnight for word from Tracy, they drove to Dallas. Courtney had suggested flying, but Mike said he'd like to have his patrol car. Its two-way radio provided fast, efficient communication. Within seconds he could be patched in to both the San Antonio and Dallas police departments.

Courtney hadn't argued. They were doing something, taking some kind of action, and that was important. It eased her anxiety somewhat.

Mike was concentrating on driving through the heavy morning traffic while she sat listening to the squawk and hum of the radio and the sounds of the road. Finally she leaned her head back against the seat sleepily. Last night, her concern for Tracy had left her able to sleep only fitfully. This morning, the movement of the car was relaxing her. She closed her eyes.

Soon Courtney was dreaming of Tracy. The girl was beside her and they were running along a white sandy beach toward Chris, who was waiting at the water's edge, her arms outstretched in welcome. Tracy flew into her mother's arms and the two embraced happily. And then she saw him, waiting a few yards farther down the beach, a smile lighting up his face, his arms open too. She ran to Mike, flinging herself into his arms, kissing him lovingly.

"Courtney. Courtney, are you awake?" Mike was shaking her arm lightly.

"Yes, umm, what?" She opened her eyes to find herself nestled against his shoulder.

"At first you were smiling. Then you laughed." He was grinning at her. "I thought you were awake." He shrugged. "I'm sorry I woke you. Here, put your head back on my shoulder."

"No, that's okay. I'm awake now."

"Come on. You need the rest." She smiled and leaned her head against his shoulder. She was still groggy, and it helped kill the time until they reached Dallas.

The scent of him, a combination of soap and a woodsy after-shave was comforting. His sports coat felt rough against her cheek, and she was terribly aware of him now, aware of his strong, hard body against hers. It reminded her of the night before, and how much she'd been tempted to reach out to him and pull him down on the bed with her.

It made no sense, but she found herself obsessed with two concerns: her fear for Tracy and her confusion about Mike. She tried to put all thoughts of Tracy from her mind, knowing that worrying couldn't help at this point. Instead she tried to analyze her feelings about Mike. She squeezed her eyes shut.

He'd worked his way into her fantasies, tormented her with his mysterious ways and tantalized her with his sensuous kisses.

He wasn't one man. He was many, and each one added a new dimension to Mike Harris. She found herself irresistibly drawn to him, despite the differences that existed between them.

But she was playing a dangerous game with herself, pursuing something she wasn't sure of, desiring experiences that might bring her unhappiness. She hadn't meant for things to develop as they had. She hadn't been aware of how deeply she had allowed herself to become involved.

He was a policeman. She knew that a man like him could demonstrate charm and likability while concealing anger and the threat of violence. Even now, after all they'd shared, she still wasn't sure of Mike. She still found herself wanting to test him, wanting to provoke him to see how long it would take before he showed his rage.

He had said once that he wanted to share his feelings, to be honest with her. But he'd said it only once, and he'd never followed through. He'd shared no more of himself after that night.

Right now, sitting here with her head on his shoulder, she wasn't sure whether he'd come along with her because he cared for her or because he thought it was his duty to do so.

"What did your captain say when you asked for a few days off?" she murmured, deciding conversation would help suppress her confused thoughts.

"He was pleased. For many reasons."

Mike recalled what his captain had said. "Taking off? That's great. You never take any time off, and God knows you need it. You're not going to work on this runaway case? That's not time off, man. You need rest. Oh, well, at least you'll be getting out of town."

"Many reasons?" She was curious.

"Yeah, mainly because I'll be out of his hair. I've been bugging him about the increased number of family disturbances we've been having. I think the policemen's union needs to come out in support of the new women's shelter the mayor's proposing. I think we should go before the city council and give them some examples of the kind of family arguments we're most often called to, and then explain that most of the time the wife is the victim and has no place to go.''

Courtney listened. She couldn't help wishing everyone in her family could hear him.

"What about you? I didn't intend it, but I overheard your conversation with your boss. I take it he didn't like the fact that you were going to Dallas.'' From what he'd heard, he suspected he was putting it mildly.

She laughed. "Nope. He said if I wanted to keep my job, I had better have my copy for the first article of my series on his desk by five o'clock Wednesday afternoon.'' She shook her head. "And he added that it had better be damned good.''

"Have you written it?'' He took the Dallas cutoff, heading north.

"I've started. But it's a tricky beginning.'' She slid across the seat and looked at him, noticing the way he sat hunched over the steering wheel, intense, purposeful. It seemed to her that he was never more comfortable than when he was working. His job was his life. How could she properly portray his intensity in her article?

"Why?''

"Because it's about you,'' she answered truthfully.

"Me?''

"Yes. I decided I'd start the series with you as the lead. You'll be interesting to my readers.''

He shook his head. "I can't imagine my being interesting."

"You don't see yourself as a hero. My readers will."

"I'm no hero," he cautioned her, glancing her way for a second before turning his attention back to the congested highway. "In the next few minutes I want you to take that Dallas map out of the glove compartment and look up your sister's address. We'll start with her house first."

"Do you think Tracy will be there?"

"I doubt it, but we might find something that will give us some idea where she is. Like I told you, from what she wrote in her diary I wouldn't be surprised to find her still in Dallas. I think there had to have been a makeup case that she decided at the last minute not to check. No girl travels without makeup, but we didn't find any in her luggage. That makes me think she acted on a whim. Left the airline ticket counter and headed back home or to one of her friends'."

"I hope so." She took the map out of the glove compartment and started looking at it.

Having Mike with her had eased Courtney's panic, and while she was still upset about her niece's disappearance, his assurance that he'd help find her had made her feel much better. When they'd left San Antonio that morning, Mike had told her that he thought Tracy would probably be easy to find.

Courtney had to believe him. She allowed herself no other theories. The alternatives were too grim.

She decided the best way to take her mind off Tracy was to get Mike to tell her about himself. Work always helped her forget her problems. Maybe she could pull something out of him that she could use in her article. "Tell me about your worst experience since you've been a police negotiator," she said.

He frowned. "There are too many to recall." Remembering meant reliving the experience. He didn't want to do that.

"Off the top of your head, what was the worst?"

"The worst—" He hesitated. "I guess the worst was when a man had barricaded himself inside his house. He had enough ammunition to blow the house down. I spent all day crouching behind a police car trying to talk to him through a bullhorn. We didn't know it, but one by one he'd killed his entire family. When we finally stormed the house, he killed himself. If I'd had any idea what he was doing, we could have gone in right away, maybe saved someone, anyway." His voice dropped almost to a whisper. "It was a bad guess on my part."

"How can you—" She was sputtering. "You act as though you blame yourself."

"I guess guilt goes with the territory."

"Rage and fury too, I bet," she said quietly.

He didn't speak. His face took on a grim expression. His eyes narrowed.

"Which way to your sister's house?"

There was no more conversation between them except the directions she gave him to the wide, highly overpriced, tree-lined streets of Highland Park.

When they pulled up to her sister's antebellum-styled house, she was weak and trembling. Could Tracy be inside?

The house was locked up tight, and no one answered the doorbell, but Mike went around to the back, crossed the brick patio and used a tool that looked to Courtney like a Boy Scout knife to pry open one of the French doors facing the immaculately tended yard. A six-foot brick fence afforded them all the privacy they needed. She followed him, not knowing what they were doing or why.

He listened, but no burglar alarm sounded. He figured the girl might have returned to the house after her mother left and disconnected it. Otherwise he would have had the entire area police force down on them by now.

When he ushered her inside they were greeted by complete silence. Slowly and silently they made their way through the downstairs rooms.

Each room was filled with expensive European antiques. Courtney had never been aware of how wealthy her sister was.

Upstairs, Tracy's room was decorated in lavender lace and satin bows. It was a teenage girl's dream room, Courtney thought, as she opened the closet and saw row after row of beautiful clothes hanging neatly. There was a color TV, a VCR, an immense stereo system and a pink telephone. The girl obviously had everything she could want.

Watching Mike as he searched through Tracy's chest of drawers made her uneasy. "What are you looking for?"

"Friends' names, notes, anything that will give us a clue where she might be. Why don't you go to your sister's room and look for a telephone number or something."

She did so, but felt overwhelmed by the massive, elegantly decorated room. The entire episode unnerved her.

"I couldn't find anything," she said after she'd given the bedroom a hasty search and returned to find Mike reading something he'd found in Tracy's chest of drawers. "What's that?"

"A list of phone numbers. Maybe it's of girlfriends or something. The names are girls' names, anyhow."

"Let's go, Mike," Courtney said nervously.

He looked up at her, frowning. "Okay. Right. Just another minute or two."

"I'll be downstairs," she said, and walked out of the room.

She waited in the back yard, where she watched two cardinals splashing in a marble bird bath. The silence outside disturbed her, too. Everything about being in her sister's house with no one there made her uneasy. She couldn't wait to get away.

When Mike appeared, he said, "We'll go get a bite to eat. It's almost two o'clock now. Then we'll pay a visit to her school principal."

Grateful to have him there making decisions for her, Courtney jumped into the car, eager to leave the tomblike house.

They found a restaurant, ordered the luncheon special and ate without a great deal of conversation. Courtney felt too tense to talk, almost too tense to eat, but Mike encouraged her to try.

When they arrived at the school, which looked as impressive as the homes they'd passed on the way, they followed the signs to the principal's office.

Mr. Towers, the principal, listened as they told him their reason for coming and then shook his head, "I'm very sorry about all of this," he said. "It's unfortunate that some of our students, despite their advantages, find themselves in trouble with the law."

"Oh, she's not in trouble with the law," Courtney protested.

"If she's skipped school and run away from home, I'd say she's in trouble, wouldn't you?" Mr. Towers replied, a bit icily.

"Was she in attendance today?" Mike asked.

"I'll check."

"I don't like him," Courtney whispered after he'd left the room.

"The man doesn't like problems. He probably sees them as a reflection upon himself," Mike said matter-of-factly.

"I bet you're right," she said, admiring Mike's skills of observation.

When he returned, he was smiling. "Well, we have no problem here," the man said. "She was in school all day from start to finish."

Mike looked up at the clock on the office wall. "How long has school been out?"

"About thirty-five minutes."

"Do you think she might still be around here?" Courtney asked, but Mike was already up and stalking out the door.

"Thanks for your help," he called back to the principal. "If we need you we'll be in touch."

Courtney ran after him. "Maybe we can find her. Oh, Mike, I hope she still looks like that picture."

"Easy to find," he said, breaking into a run toward the front of the building where they'd seen clusters of students when they'd come in.

"Why?"

He snapped his fingers at her and smiled. "Your blue eyes. She has your blue eyes."

He was feeling as happy as she was, Courtney decided as she ran to catch up with him. Tracy had been here. Nothing bad had happened to her. She hadn't been abducted. Courtney shut away her ugly thoughts. Her niece had been in school today.

Mike searched the faces of the students. When he saw no sign of her, he walked up to a group. "Say, any of you know Tracy Blume?"

"Yeah," one of the boys said.

"Any of you see her today?"

"She wasn't in school today," the boy told him. The others in the group nodded their agreement.

"You sure?"

"I'm sure. Tracy wasn't here."

Mike whipped around and ran back toward the principal's office. Courtney had caught up with him just in time to hear the kids say they hadn't seen Tracy.

Slowly, Courtney retraced her steps. But when she was halfway down the hallway, Mike stormed toward her.

"She wasn't here. The principal made a mistake. He had a different Tracy in mind. One who's usually in trouble, he said." Mike shook his head. "Tracy never showed up today."

It was no use. She couldn't do anything to dam up the tears that spilled out then. She began to cry softly.

He took her in his arms and led her back to the car. When they were inside, he held her close to him, using his left hand to retrieve his two-way radio and place several calls. "I have to drive to the police station," he said. "It's only a few blocks from here."

She waited in the car for a very long time while he went inside. When he came back he said he'd advised the police departments in San Antonio and Dallas to put out a full alert for Tracy.

Courtney didn't listen to the rest of the details of the arrangements he'd made. Things seemed to be getting worse instead of better. She was so overwhelmed by emotion that she found it impossible to dry her tears. She'd thought that after last night she'd used them all up, but it seemed they were coming from some inexhaustible source.

She retrieved Tracy's diary from her purse. Opening it, she stared hard at the girl's photograph, and recalled Tracy as a tiny, happy child.

Mike was talking on the radio again, but when he was finished with his business, he took her chin in his hand and lifted it toward him. "Hey," he whispered, "we can't get discouraged now. This is just a setback, a temporary setback."

"What—what are we going to do now?" she cried.

"First, we're going to find a nice motel. We're going to call and check in with your friend who's staying in your apartment. Then we'll call your mother and check back with the police to give them a number where they can reach us tonight. After that, I'm going to tuck you in for the night, and then I'm going to start contacting the names on this list. But first you've got to stop crying. It doesn't look good for a lovely woman to be seen crying in my car. People will think I've done something awful to you."

She tried to respond to his teasing with a smile, and nearly succeeded. "Okay." She blew her nose, and struggled for self-control.

Evening had fallen, and Mike drove in the darkness until he came to an attractive-looking motel, asked for her opinion, and waited to go in until he had her approval.

Courtney held her breath, wondering what kind of arrangements he would make. Upset, confused, she didn't know what she'd say if he expected her to share a room.

But he came back to the car with two keys in his hand, and she felt a curious mingling of relief and regret.

She tried to suppress her wildly swinging emotions. "Why am I so tired?" she asked in a tight voice.

"Stress. You're upset."

"I feel like a bear in hibernation. I'm so tired."

"Get as much rest as you can," he told Courtney as he led her to her room, carrying her suitcase for her. "I'm going to be in the adjoining room. I'll bring you something to eat later."

"Oh, no, that's all right," she said.

He caught her nervousness. "I'll bring it in and leave it if you like."

"I didn't mean—"

"I know exactly what you meant." He looked at her intensely. "Courtney, when this is over you and I are going to have a talk, but for now, let me tell you you don't have to worry. I have no intention of coming in here and seducing you."

And that is probably my loss, she said to herself, immensely embarrassed by his comments. Aloud she said, "I think I'll take you up on your suggestion about resting."

"I'll be right next door. Let me know if you need me."

If I need you, she thought. Hadn't she been demonstrating how much she needed him? Hadn't he had enough, this man who'd proclaimed that he wanted no complications?

She called Mary Claire first, and then her mother. Neither of them had anything to report, and so the conversations were very brief. Then Courtney took a long hot bath, put on her pink silk kimono and stretched out on the bed.

She put her hand across her forehead, lying there in the darkness, wishing her life could magically revert to the way it had been a week before. She began to cry, but stopped herself, refusing to give in to self-pity any longer. Instead she went into the bathroom, reapplied her makeup and brushed her hair.

Later, when Mike knocked softly at the door that connected their rooms, she was sitting up in bed, working on her article. "Please come in," she said, thankful for the interruption. The article was proving more and more difficult. She couldn't get a grasp on what she wanted to say about Mike.

He brought hot roast beef sandwiches, milk and coffee. They ate sitting at a corner table that was too high to be comfortable, yet was more manageable than sitting on the bed.

While they ate, he gave her a rundown of the little he'd found out. The names on the list had proved to be Tracy's girlfriends, but he'd gotten no real information from any of them, and had been unable to contact several of them. Those were the ones, he promised her, they'd begin with the next morning.

"You still think she's here with friends?" Courtney asked, praying he'd say yes.

"I'm still going on that assumption. The girl didn't want to come to San Antonio." He shook his head. "I got the name of a boyfriend, a sometime boyfriend, one of the girls' mother called him. We'll pay him a visit tomorrow, too."

"Does he go to school with her?"

"No. He's out of school. Working at a gas station near her house."

Courtney nodded and began cleaning up the mess from their meal. A yawn escaped her. She couldn't stop it.

"I'd better let you get some sleep," he said, getting up to leave.

She followed him to the door, and just before he opened it she said, "Mike, whatever your reasons for helping me, I want you to know I'm extremely grateful."

He turned to face her. "My reason," he replied curtly, "is you."

"I'd like to believe that."

"Then do."

He saw the doubt in her eyes, but he felt no anger, only regret.

He was tempted, painfully tempted, to take her into his arms and kiss away her mistrust. But if he did, he knew he'd be unable to release her.

He didn't want to do anything now to disturb her. He knew he should simply leave, but he couldn't.

She looked so tempting. Her lips were wet, parted in unconscious invitation. Her hair was loose and shining. The silky kimono she was wearing clung to the curves of her breasts in the most tempting way.

He was going to kiss her. In an instant, the longing had become too intense for him to bear.

He bent his head. Her eyes closed in expectation, and then his lips were on hers, his pulse pounding. He held her with trembling hands and caressed her tenderly.

Giving her what he hoped was the gentlest of kisses, Mike decided she tasted of fresh mint. Her honeyed sweetness sent his body clamoring for more.

Their lips met, parted, came together again, this time passionately. It had to end. He knew that. He knew what would happen if he continued to taste the sweetness of her lips. If he didn't release her, he would have to touch her in more intimate ways.

But he didn't want to give up this taste of heaven. He found he couldn't.

She tried to pull away, but his strong arms held her fast. Her heart was hammering loudly. She could feel the tension building in his body. She knew she couldn't back out now, not with his arms wrapped around her so tightly, his mouth so tantalizingly persuasive.

"Don't leave me now," he murmured, his voice harsh with emotion.

As if from some far-off place she heard him speak, felt the warmth of his breath upon her cheek. Then when he began to kiss her again, gently yet forcefully, she felt lost to his power, and her tiredness vanished completely.

And as his tongue pressed insistently against her own, she knew that she wanted nothing to interfere with the sensations coursing through her body. At this instant she imagined herself a rocket gone awry.

He scooped her up into his arms, and brushed her lips with his. The tenderness of his kiss melted the remnants of her resistance into nothingness.

She was shaking, speechless, and she wanted him, needed him more than she'd ever needed anything in her life.

With a swift glance that seemed to peer directly into her soul, he took two long strides to the bed. After he put her down he smiled gently, as if to reassure her. He brushed away a wayward strand of hair that had fallen across her face.

Mike felt her tension as she stood before him. Then his hand slid caressingly over her throat, stroking her lovingly until the tension eased. Moving so slowly that Courtney almost couldn't bear it, he slid the silk kimono inch by inch off her shoulders.

"You're beautiful," he whispered when, as if in a trance, she moved her hands down to her side so that she could finally rid herself of the robe. He pushed it away, sending it floating to the floor. Then he moved his hands down her rib cage in restless exploration and then upward until he had caught the top of her gown with his fingers and could slide it down across her breasts and dispose of it in the same way he'd disposed of the kimono. He put his hand on her hip, and she gasped. "You're so beautiful," he whispered once more.

Courtney stood immobile, entranced by his touch. He gave her a new awareness of her own body and the sensations that could be awakened in it. Never having experienced anything that could compare to this, she gave herself completely to the feeling.

When his hands circled warmly over her flat abdomen, her own involuntarily flew to his hard chest. A hint of a smile played across her face. She seemed to be enjoying his every touch, his lightest caress, and he continued his exploration, becoming bolder as he did.

Then, when her fingers tangled in the hair on his chest, he felt himself shudder and thought for a moment he'd lose control. A sigh broke from his lips, and he pulled back from her slightly.

He kissed her again, once more savoring her warmth and her taste. Then, tenderly, as if she were infinitely fragile, he lowered her to the bed. When he lay down beside her she tried to tell him how perfect she believed this to be, how perfectly their bodies fit together, her head nestled against the broad expanse of his shoulder, her breasts touching the coarse hair on his chest, but words failed her. The only sound that issued from her throat was a moan of desire.

They lay together, their arms and legs entwined, kissing, exploring each other's bodies, murmuring sounds only they could understand. Courtney realized that this moment had been inevitable from the first. They'd stalked each other like creatures of the jungle, each the hunter, each the hunted, until this moment had finally arrived.

Now, as much as she wanted the experience to be quick and full of the heated passion she'd held at bay so long, she also wanted to make certain she savored each moment, each movement. For the two of them, she realized, there was no future, no past. Only the present mattered.

Mike brought her breast to his lips and kissed it. With his tongue he traced the nipple's outline until Courtney felt as if she might burst with excitement.

He teased her nipples for long minutes with his tongue. Finally he took one of the hard buds into his mouth, tormenting it with his teeth, sending shock waves of desire from her breast throughout her entire body.

His lips wove a slow, moist trail upward along her throat, seeking her warm mouth. When he found it he quickly took possession of it, thrilled to feel her tongue pushing hungrily against his. But then he pulled away, slightly, slowly.

She opened her eyes. She waited. When he made no move she acted, reaching out to pull him to her with shaking hands. Her mouth sought his, urgent, demanding.

He reveled in the assurance her actions gave him, and as if the final barrier between them had fallen, his hands began an exploration intended to leave no part of her body untouched.

Courtney writhed in ecstasy, and a beautiful heat engulfed her. His fingers slid down along the curve of her hips, then inward to her thighs.

Finally he rose over her, and their bodies moved against one another in total abandon. It seemed that each was at the limit of endurance. They were caught up in the power of the explosion that was thundering through them.

They shared a shuddering climax that left them weak and gasping and clinging to each other desperately.

Later he took her again, pulling her into his arms, pressing hard against her, touching her, kissing her until they were both senseless, hungry, wanting. They clung to one another, burning in the white-hot flames of desire.

And then they rested. He kept his arm around her so that she was nestled against him. They were exhausted, but there was a glow to their exhaustion, a satisfied glow.

Together they slept, their arms entwined. It was the first undisturbed sleep for both of them in days.

Sometime in the early morning hours, Courtney put her hand out to touch him, but came away with nothing. She opened her eyes. He'd gone, leaving her only the memories of his smooth skin and the way he had made love to her with such tenderness.

Chapter Eight

Sunlight poured across Mike's bed, and he shielded his eyes from the harsh morning rays. He yawned, rubbed his face with his hands, and then broke into a wide smile.

He looked around the room as if afraid he might be observed. But he was alone. He remembered leaving the comforting warmth of Courtney's bed and going into his own room. It had been almost daybreak. He had kissed her on the forehead and bid her a quiet goodbye so as not to wake her.

He lay back against the sheets and let his mind wander, sifting the events of the night before. It had all been spectacular. Again he smiled. He believed

Kelly glanced at her mother. "Yes, sir. I sure will."

As they drove away from the French home, Courtney said, "I knew Tracy wouldn't be running away."

Mike started laughing. "Oh, really?"

She looked at him. Then she laughed too. "Well, I hoped she wouldn't," Courtney said, relief washing over her in great waves.

"Well, I'm just glad things are turning out this way." Mike was trying to follow the directions Mrs. French had given for the McAfree home. "And I don't want you to get your hopes up. We may have to wait for her to come back from the coast tomorrow—if she's really gone down there."

After interviewing Mrs. McAfree and then talking to Mrs. Barnes in her home, they were convinced that the three girls had indeed gone to the coast. Both Mrs. McAfree and Mrs. Barnes claimed not to know what their daughters were doing. Mrs. Barnes owned a beach house in Corpus Christi, and Mike decided the girls had probably gone there.

He immediately radioed a request to have a Corpus Christi police car go by and check on the girls, but again Mike warned the patrolmen not to disturb them. A few hours later word came back that they were there.

"If she intends to contact you, if she's already told her friends she will, then it might be better to let her carry out her plan," he said as the two of them sat in the car outside a restaurant.

"No," Courtney said. "I want to see her."

But Mike insisted. "The child is rebelling. Why not let her get it out of her system? It looks like she's got plenty to rebel about, and maybe she's not handling it well by acting out like this, but at least she's planning on coming back to you."

"So says that...Kelly whatever-her-name-is."

"She's safe. We know where she is. She's going to be fine. If you let her come to you on her own terms, she'll be working out a way to handle her problems. Maybe not the way we think she should, but she's trying. I think it would be best for you to let her walk through this her way." Memories of his childhood flashed before him, memories he'd never shared with anyone. "Just be there for her when she comes out of this thing. That's the best advice I can give you."

"But I have to go back to San Antonio tomorrow. I can't wait around for her," Courtney said.

"Yes, I know."

"What should I do? I can't leave her here."

"But you have to. Trust me. I'll put you on a plane. When she calls you—and I'll bet a thousand bucks she does—I'll pick her up and drive her to San Antonio. It'll put the fear of God into her to have a police escort. Have faith, Courtney. I'll take care of everything."

She winced. "I can't leave."

He reached across the car seat and pulled her into his arms. "You want to keep your job. This series is important to you." He paused, then tucked his finger beneath her chin. "I want to help you, Courtney. You wouldn't be doing anything here that I can't handle alone. This is my business, remember? I'll have someone following those girls every step of the way back from Corpus Christi. If she doesn't try to contact you right away, I'll pick her up immediately." He ran his hands through his hair and looked straight into her eyes. "I'm asking you to put your faith in me. Is that asking too much?"

Suddenly they seemed to be talking about something very important. All her years of mistrust of men in uniform were on the line. She knew it, and felt that he could sense it, also.

"All right," she said shakily.

Putting her faith in Mike was something that took conviction as well as hope. Courtney was happy to realize she had both.

She might end up getting hurt, she warned herself. But she was going to take the chance. She agreed to do as he'd suggested, and they spent their dinner discussing the psychological pressures a teenager like Tracy had to go through. She admired the knowledge Mike seemed to have of psychology and people. She only wished he'd share a little of himself the way he shared his understanding of the human condition.

After dinner they went back to the motel. When they entered her room, she could feel the nervous energy surging between them. She considered inviting him to stay, and could tell that he was thinking along the same lines.

As Mike waited expectantly, Courtney searched for an easy way to let him know she didn't want him to leave.

But abruptly, without looking at her, he swung around and was out the door. "I'll talk to you later," he called back over his shoulder.

She followed him to the door and locked it behind him, knowing what he'd been going through. She'd gone through the same thing. Neither of them had been able to find the words, the gestures, the expressions to communicate their needs.

For a moment she leaned against the door. Her sudden loss of speech had surprised her. It wasn't like her not to have the words she needed. She thought of him, and the way he so carefully skirted personal conversation, personal expression.

If she went to him now, would he welcome her? The urge to try sent her racing across the room to the connecting door, but then she paused. Hold back, she told herself. Hold back.

She took a shower and then opened her briefcase. Maybe it would be better to spend the evening writing about him than thinking about him, she tried to tell her lonely heart.

* * *

She was in the other room, barely six feet away.

He tore at his shirt and stripped off his clothes. Suddenly hot. Too hot.

He stood under the shower, turning the spray as cold and as strong as it would go. He bent his head, letting the water flow over it. After a few minutes, he realized it was doing no good.

He got out, dried himself off and threw on a pair of pajama bottoms. He began pacing the floor.

Knowing that she was so close was driving him insane. He was drawn irresistibly to the door that separated them. He knocked once, then again, harder the second time.

"Come in," she answered, so softly Mike could hardly hear her voice.

Throwing the door open, he stepped inside. She was sitting up in bed leaning against the headboard, working. Papers were strewn around her in a disorderly semicircle. Her arm was poised as she sat writing what he assumed was her article.

When he entered, she pushed the papers aside and sat watching his approach. Still in the shadows, he willed himself to imagine her expectant, waiting, her breath coming in shallow little gasps. He imagined the whisper of her breath, and the soft, warm feel of her pale skin. He was like a man possessed.

At the foot of the bed he stopped. Over the course of the day he had warned himself not to want her as he did, so badly that his entire body was tense with desire. He'd told himself not to need her the way his mind was trying to trick him into thinking he did.

But it was as if he had no will of his own. He was ready to do her bidding, intent upon pleasing her, awakening in her the same volcanic heat he was experiencing.

"Mike," she whispered.

"Yes." He leaned forward, tossing aside the sheet that covered her. He gazed longingly at her body, and then his eyes met hers. She was wearing a nightgown of winter-white chiffon.

He paused, not touching her. "Am I welcome here?" His voice sounded hoarse and uncontrolled.

"Yes," she said simply.

Courtney had let go the night before, had responded to the moment and to her emotions. Events had swept her along, and now she was tied to him, in love with him.

Tonight, she would again let herself go—accept the reality and the man. Tonight, despite her worry over Tracy, she had what she wanted: Mike.

He reached out to caress her throat, his thumbs sliding downward along her collarbone. Carefully he eased himself down to the edge of the bed, where he sat facing her.

When his hands began to roam, he found the chiffon nightgown she was wearing a hindrance. Without a moment's hesitation he reached up to slip the satin straps of the gown off her shoulders. His eyes on hers, he allowed his fingers to follow the satin straps as they descended from her warm shoulders along the soft curve of her arms.

She shivered, and Mike smiled, pleased to see her reaction to his touch. Bending forward, he kissed her throat, then let his lips follow the trail of the gown from her shoulders down across her breasts and finally to her waist. Again he felt her respond with an internal tremor, and it pleased him, as did the clean scent of her perfume and the creamy softness of her skin.

Her hands came up to encircle his head, her fingers weaving their way through his dark, thick hair. He felt his scalp tingle with anticipation.

Bunched around her waist, the gown could be slid no further. He lifted her slightly, cupping his hands just below her buttocks so that he could easily strip the chiffon away from her body. All the while his lips followed the path of the gown. His warm mouth traveled from her stomach to her thigh, and then moved on to her legs and feet. He wanted to brand every inch of her body with his kiss.

Raising his head at last, he gave her a long, passion-filled stare. He turned out the lamp on the bedside table, and then brought his lips to hers. Her mouth was warm and eager.

He kissed her lightly and moved next to her. As he was pressing against her, he deepened his kiss and allowed his hand to move leisurely down to caress her breast. Her arm came up to settle around his wide shoulders.

As one, they slid down to the center of the bed. He wanted to feel the full length of her body against his own. He caressed her hip, urging her closer, urging her to bridge the little distance that still separated them.

He felt her fingers moving tentatively along the length of his spine. Their fluttering touch stopped at the waistband of his pajamas, then began to slip between fabric and flesh.

Unable to resist, he immediately reached down and disposed of the bothersome pajamas himself. He felt her hand moving along the ridge of his hip, exploring with a feather-light touch. He had to bite his lip to keep from crying out. The intimacy of her touch was driving him mad.

Lovingly yet possessively he caressed her legs. He heard her catch her breath, but then she began to respond with a thorough exploration of her own.

Their kisses were passionate, desperate. Their tongues danced and dueled, wildly and shamelessly.

Each was the prisoner of the other, and they were held together by tangled limbs and quivering need. Hungrily he explored the flatness of her belly, the slight swell of her thigh, the heat of her womanhood.

Arching uncontrollably toward him she moaned, urging him on as he wedged his knee between her thighs and raised himself over her.

His mouth moved to tease her breasts as he raised her to meet the thrust of his consuming need. When they were united, they began to move in rhythmic unison.

Locking her arms around his neck, she thrust her body wantonly against his. She clenched her teeth, moaning, pushing against him so that her lips met his sweat-covered shoulder.

He felt her teeth on his flesh and heard the sound of her voice as she whimpered. Together they were riding upward through the wind into a raging, whirling cyclone.

She had no thought of anything but the driving frenzy within her. Hearing him groan, she opened her eyes in time to see his face tense with the power of his climax, and then she was soaring toward her own, shuddering toward a final all-consuming release.

"Oh, Mike, I love you," she cried as she floated high on the clouds of ecstasy. She sailed away and over the brink of consciousness, giving all of her being over to the fires of primal response.

"Let me hold you," he whispered as he eased down beside her, still breathing hard, but taking her eagerly into his arms.

When their lovemaking had finally released them, Courtney turned away from him, feigning sleep. But she remained awake, even when his breath grew steady and rhythmic and she was sure he was asleep.

She had made a tremendous mistake. She'd told him she loved him, had confessed to Mike what she wasn't comfortable voicing even to herself.

The fact that he had not answered her except to express the wish to comfort her was disturbing. Could she have been correct in her initial assessment?

She moved to her side of the bed and lay there, looking over at Mike. He lay on his side, his hand extended across the bed as if he were reaching to make contact with her. She found she wanted him again, yearned to be held tenderly in his strong arms, and the realization did little to ease the regret in her heart.

Pity, sympathy, understanding, compassion. That was what he felt for her. That was all he'd been offering all along.

He'd warned her. Friendship was all he'd wanted. He'd been as good as his word.

A single tear spilled onto the bed. In the stillness of the night, Courtney felt as if she could hear her heart. It sounded as if it were breaking.

Chapter Nine

As soon as you hear something you call me at this number,'' Mike said the next morning as he drove her to the airport. "I'll have a tail on her, but I want to give her a chance to contact you."

Courtney took the card with the phone number on it.

"They'll patch you right through to me."

She nodded. "Very well," she said, not looking at him.

She had gotten up before six and spent an hour in the bathroom, taking a shower and washing her hair. She'd waited until Mike had returned to his room to dress before she had come out of the bathroom.

After her confession of love had fallen on deaf ears the night before, she'd decided that seeing him in the intimacy of her bed would be too painful. She didn't want any reminders of the embarrassment she'd caused herself.

"I don't want to leave," she said quietly.

Taken by surprise, he looked at her. There was a firmness around her mouth that he'd come to recognize as an indication of just how stubborn she could get.

"But in the interest of keeping your job, you have to," he replied.

"I—"

"You said you trusted me."

She felt his eyes on her. There was a long pause before she answered him. "I did say that. I remember."

Maybe it was childish of her, she thought. Maybe she should be handling herself in a more adult way, but she couldn't. She was hurt, bruised by his lack of response to her. She couldn't be cheery or talkative this morning, and everything suddenly seemed ominous to her again.

Suppose things didn't work out. Suppose Tracy didn't come back. Suppose she didn't call as she'd told her friend she would. There were too many possibilities for Courtney to handle.

"Trust me," he said. "I'll take care of everything."

Like you took care of stealing my heart, she thought. But that wasn't being honest, Courtney admitted. She'd given him her heart. He hadn't asked for it. She'd thrust it at him, forgetting that he didn't want it at all.

As he turned into the airport parking lot, he too was thinking about the night before. She'd said she loved him. He'd been so overwhelmed that he'd been speechless. It seemed everything had happened at once.

Now he wanted to talk about it with her, but she was as aloof as he'd ever seen her. Something was wrong, and there was no time to resolve anything now. He had only five minutes to get her on the plane to San Antonio.

They said their goodbyes. Mike tried to kiss her, but she turned her head at the last minute, and he brushed his lips against her cool cheek. He hated it, wanted to grab her and kiss her unrelentingly until she revealed what she was feeling. But he didn't. Instead, he stood stoically by as she boarded the plane.

He tried to tell himself that she was upset because she was leaving without her niece. But he wasn't as convinced of that as he'd have liked to be. He was worried now. When would he have the chance to tell her how he felt about her?

All the way back to San Antonio, as the flight attendants passed up and down the aisle offering drinks in small plastic cups, Courtney sat staring miserably out the thick window at a leaden sky.

Somehow her life had fallen apart in a matter of days.

First, Tracy had disappeared. Then she'd given her body and soul to Mike, and found that instead of returning her love, he'd only been feeling sympathetic to her needs and attempting to ease her pain in any way he could.

Now she was on her way to an office and a boss who would be very angry if she didn't immediately hand over the first article of her series. Inside her briefcase, on a heavily edited piece of paper, she had two brief paragraphs written. Who could write while experiencing the kind of emotional upheaval she was living through?

When she heard the flight attendant announce their impending landing in San Antonio, Courtney buckled her seat belt and glanced down at her briefcase. She had vowed she'd write on the way. She hadn't even opened the case. A heavy weight sank down to the pit of her stomach and settled there, and she was afraid the feeling would remain for quite some time to come.

Once back in San Antonio, she made a quick trip to her apartment and called her sister Chris in Europe. Chris told her she'd be home very soon and assured her that Tracy was a levelheaded girl, even though it might not look that way right now. A little surprised at Chris's response, Courtney told her she'd call as soon as she heard anything. Meanwhile, Chris said she'd be arranging for a weekend flight back to Texas. As soon as she hung up, Courtney headed for the newspaper office.

"Oh, Courtney, you've got to tell me all about what's been happening," Mary Claire exclaimed when Courtney had settled back into her office.

"I'm sorry, Mary Claire, but right now I don't have the time. I haven't seen Tracy, but we know where she is. Mike will probably be bringing her home this afternoon." She tried to smile at her friend. "Do I have any messages?" It was too early for her to hear from Tracy, but she was hoping.

"No," Mary Claire said thoughtfully. "Unless you count those on the intercom. Mr. Wagner's on the warpath because you haven't been here this week. Says you'd better have a Pulitzer Prize-winning article ready for him by five o'clock."

Courtney raised her eyes to the wall clock that hung over the main door of the office. "Is that thing correct?"

Mary Claire nodded. "Do you have it ready?"

Courtney sighed. "'Fraid not."

"Want me to help?"

Courtney thought of the two skimpy paragraphs she'd completed. "I don't think so. Not that I don't appreciate it, but..." Her voice trailed off.

"That bad, huh? Are you blocked?"

"I guess."

"Why don't you go into Mr. Delgado's office. He's out for the afternoon. Hole up in there and work, if you can."

Mary Claire and Courtney simultaneously glanced at the clock. Courtney had an hour and thirty-eight minutes before she was due in Mr. Wagner's office. She'd need a miracle to get her article written in time.

"Okay," she said with a sigh. "I'll try."

"Anything you need, call me."

That was one thing in her favor, Courtney told herself as she hurried to the vacant office. Mary Claire had come through for her like a champ. The moment she'd explained her predicament, and that she had "this policeman friend" who would be helping her, Mary Claire hadn't been able to do enough for her. She was just like the old friend she'd once been, and it warmed Courtney's heart.

"What I need most," Courtney said when she reached the office door, "is to know that my niece is safe and sound." *And to have my love returned by Mike,* she added silently.

"We'll hear soon," Mary Claire answered with a smile of encouragement. "And it will be good news."

"Yeah," Courtney said softly before closing the door behind her.

Ignoring her surroundings, she propped her brief-case up on the desk and took out what she'd written. She sat staring at the words, conjuring up pictures in her head.

The only way she would be able to write this article would be if she knew Tracy was safe and sound and if she could get some emotional distance from the topic at hand. But how could she ignore what she felt in her heart?

She'd changed her mind about the focus of her series, or rather Mike had changed her mind for her. He'd shown her that a policeman could be forceful and compellingly tough, yet warm and responsive at the same time.

She'd originally planned to write her series about the negative aspects of police work. Firsthand experience had changed her mind.

Now she was worried that the man, the flesh-and-blood character, would get in her way. Yet wasn't that what first-class journalism actually was—making words come alive, so powerfully that they portrayed real people, actual happenings? If only she could regain her objectivity, she felt she could pull it off, create the miracle.

She sat staring down at the words she'd written. They seemed foreign, carrying no meaning for her now. She blinked, rubbed her eyes and tried again.

"Courtney, line one for you," Mary Claire cried, bursting into the room. "I've got my fingers crossed. It's a female voice."

"Thanks." The hope that had filled Mary Claire's voice carried over to hers. Shakily she picked up the telephone and punched the button for the first line. "Hello," she said.

"Aunt Courtney?" a girl's voice said.

Courtney's heart lurched. "Yes," she said, still filled with apprehension.

"Aunt Courtney, this is Tracy, Tracy Blume. Aunt Courtney, I'm calling to apologize." The girl's voice became weak.

"Yes," Courtney said, afraid to trust her voice just yet.

"I'm at a friend's house in Dallas, and I want to come to San Antonio now."

She remembered Mike's advice. "I've been terribly worried about you, Tracy. Terribly upset."

"Does my mother know?"

"Yes. She does."

"Did you call her?"

"Your mother and the police and your grandmother. We've all been worried about you."

"I should have called."

"Tracy, do you know what the word *understatement* means?"

"Yes," she said, a questioning tone in her voice.

"I think you just made the biggest one I ever heard."

"I'm sorry," Tracy sighed. "I should have called you."

"Yes, you should have," Courtney answered, tears choking her.

"I was upset."

"So was I." Not wanting to be too harsh, Courtney said, "So when are you coming?"

"How about today?"

"Fine. Where are you? I'll have a friend pick you up and bring you."

Courtney quickly took down Tracy's friend's address, information she already had. She talked to her niece a few more minutes, then said goodbye. "I'm looking forward to seeing you, Tracy."

"You are?"

"Why wouldn't I be?"

The girl's voice sounded very tentative. "I guess I thought you'd be so mad at me you wouldn't want to see me."

"I'd never get that mad at you. See you soon, dear."

She hung up the phone and put her head down on the desk, sighing with relief. The nightmare was over.

Then she called the number Mike had given her and was patched through to the radio in his car.

"Mike, she's at Joanna's house, waiting. I told her you'd be there to pick her up."

"Yeah, I talked to the girl's mother already. She said Tracy said she really wasn't thinking.... Well, you'll have a chance to talk to her about it all yourself later. We'll probably be at your place by nine-thirty or so.''

"That's wonderful news."

"How's the article going?"

She looked down at the paper in front of her. "It'll be fine," she said.

"Okay. See you soon. You and I need a chance to talk, too."

"Yes. I'll see you tonight."

Riding a flood tide of emotion, Courtney placed a call to her mother, tried unsuccessfully to reach Chris again in Paris and left a message saying that Tracy was fine.

At ten after four she put her briefcase on the floor and began to type. Her nerves were still frayed, and her heart was filled with gratitude and sadness. When she had written two complete sentences a flash of inspiration hit her. She began to write quickly and confidently. By four fifty-eight she was running her article off on the high-speed printer.

"The boss is calling for you," Mary Claire said, rather dramatically, as she stuck her head inside the office door.

"Be right there," Courtney called, tearing off the first copy of her article. There'd been no time for proofreading. She had to hope it was letter-perfect.

"Run," Mary Claire urged as she followed Courtney partway down the hall to the door marked Private.

"Mr. Wagner?" Courtney stepped into his office without knocking.

"Miss Evans, I presume? I wasn't sure you worked here anymore." His tone of voice was vaguely threatening. "Tell me, young lady, do you or do you not have something for me? If not, I may have something for you." He arched his brows meaningfully.

"I have something for you." She handed him her article. "I think you'll like it." Wagner was always making threats; it went along with his image. She intended to show him she wasn't shaking in her boots waiting to be fired.

"Hmm," he muttered. "I'll be the judge of that, thank you."

From office rumor and experience she knew that if he began reading her article aloud to her it meant he was really angry and was actually contemplating a firing. It was one of his best-known traits.

"'The Invincible Warrior,'" he read in a grumbling, sarcastic voice.

The words, read so critically, struck her ears like machine-gun bullets. The article sounded as if she might be trying to describe a human Superman. She talked of Mike's daily work, of the commitment he made and the effort he put forth, and when she'd written it she'd thought it sounded warm and inspiring. Hearing her boss read it aloud made her cringe.

Her cheeks grew warmer with each word he spoke. She wished she could flee the room.

When the painful ordeal was finally over she waited. Drained to the point of exhaustion, Courtney hoped he'd just get it over with, fire her, tell her she was finished.

"Tell me, Courtney, are you proud of this article of yours?" he asked finally.

"Well, uh, I was," she answered truthfully, "a few minutes ago."

"You're saying you're not now?" he demanded.

Taking a deep breath and tensing her shoulders a little, Courtney stared back at her boss. "No, sir," she answered defiantly. "I'm proud of my work."

"This?" He threw the pages at her, and she surprised herself by catching them.

"Yes." Her defiance was growing.

"I am, too," he said, lowering his gruff voice a notch or two.

She blinked. What had he said? Was she hearing things?

As if he could read her mind, he grinned, then said, "Damned good work. Now let's print it."

"As is?" she asked, still dumbfounded. She couldn't believe he wouldn't want to change something.

"Don't you think it's perfect?"

"Well . . . yes, sir," she replied with a gulp.

He grabbed for the telephone on his desk. "Get me the pressroom. Bob? Say, Bob, we've got a series by Courtney Evans starting tomorrow morning. I want you to see to it that we have a double border around it. Put her picture at the top." He stopped to listen to the man at the other end. "I'll eat my hat if we don't increase circulation with this. It's that good." He laughed. "No, I don't own a hat, but I still think it's quality work." He looked at Courtney. "Yeah, her second one will be just as good. I'll be reading it by noon tomorrow while I wait for my congratulatory calls on the first one."

Courtney shook her head, unable to believe her good fortune.

"Twelve o'clock sharp, young lady. That's when I want to see article number two. More about this fella, I suppose." He was pointing to her copy.

"Uh, yes, sir."

"Good. Now send that downstairs and let's go home."

Beaming, Courtney didn't wait around for him to change his mind. Instead, after filling Mary Claire in on what was happening, she hurried home to await Tracy and Mike's arrival.

The long trip back to San Antonio gave Mike plenty of time to talk to the girl beside him. Once she'd gotten over her initial resistance and accepted his assurance that he was a policeman who also happened to be a friend of her aunt's, Tracy had carried on a conversation with him without noticeable hesitancy. When he'd informed her that her mother would be coming back from Paris on the weekend to bring her back to Dallas, he'd been pleased to see a smile light her face.

Dressed in a pair of faded denims and a red-and-black plaid oversized shirt, her hair pulled back in a ponytail, Tracy looked like any attractive and vivacious teenager—except that she had Courtney's pale blue eyes and her smile. The resemblance was almost uncanny.

He watched her watch him. She'd made a mistake, acting on impulse, Mike believed, and while she'd made no formal apology to him, he was sure she wasn't proud of what she'd done.

She'd given him the details of her escapade, and when they'd left her friend's house she'd smiled and waved as though she were going on an outing she was looking forward to. He'd bought them both milkshakes before they left Dallas, and listened to her complain about the calories as she greedily drained the cup.

"What's your favorite rock group?" he asked. "Sorry I don't have a radio for you to listen to."

"That's okay. I've got my blaster back there." She raised her head to indicate her things in the back seat. "Group? " she answered without any hesitation. "Bananarama. Singer? Phil Collins."

"I like him too," Mike said. "Can't say that I know your group."

"They're great." She nodded, as if agreeing with herself. "So you're a friend of my aunt's."

He heard the innuendo in her question and felt her gaze on him as he drove. He forced himself to keep his eyes on the road. "Yes. We're friends."

"What sort of friends?" She smiled slyly. "I mean like friend-friends, boyfriend-girlfriend, what?"

When he heard that he couldn't help himself. He broke into a grin and glanced over at her. She was staring straight at him, and he had the feeling that it was important to give this girl a straight answer. But he wanted to test her sense of humor first.

"Nosy, aren't you?" His grin widened.

Tracy laughed. "I guess so, but whatever you tell me won't shock me."

"Oh, you're a woman of the world, huh?"

"My mother's been married three times, and she's had more boyfriends than I get Christmas presents."

There was a hardness in her voice, and Mike didn't like the sound of it.

"Boyfriend-girlfriend, I hope."

"You hope?" she began. "Then you don't live together or anything like that?"

He shook his head, his smile all but disappearing. "We've only known each other a little while."

He'd been doing some serious thinking about Courtney since he'd put her on the airplane. He knew he was carrying a lifetime's worth of emotional baggage around with him. Sharing himself with another person had always seemed too frightening a prospect until Courtney had come into his life. Now he was eager to do so. He intended to tell her that just as soon as he could.

"Funny," Tracy said, studying him intently. "My mom always told me her family didn't like co—policemen. She said it was because of my dad. She doesn't like them either. My father used to beat her."

He admired the girl's disarming forthrightness. She didn't seem to be playing games with him or trying to put him on. Instead, she impressed him as being very much like Courtney, a person filled with curiosity. It must be a family trait, he thought.

"I've heard something about that."

Tracy leaned forward, blew away a strand of dark hair that had strayed from her ponytail and looked straight at him again. "I never really understood why the family didn't like policemen. Like I said, my mother's had boyfriends by the dozens. She kept telling me with every one of them that I should judge them on their own merits."

He was amazed. If anyone had told him he'd be carrying on this kind of conversation with Courtney's niece, he'd never have believed it. The girl was one of the sharpest, most articulate sixteen-year-olds he'd ever met. "What you're saying makes sense to me," he told her.

"Yeah," she went on, sensing his interest. "I've had tennis lessons from one boyfriend of hers, and then skiing lessons from another. My mom's second husband was an English professor at SMU. He tried to make me read the classics when I was just a little kid. And then I was psychoanalyzed to pieces by her third husband. I mean," she said with a giggle, "it's like playing musical chairs at my house." She was laughing hard now.

He looked at her. He thought he saw pain behind the pale blue eyes. Wondering if he should chance making her dislike him, he decided to go for broke. "Sounds very confusing to me."

Her laughter died. "Hey, I wasn't complaining. It's funny, don't you see?"

His eyes met hers. "No, I don't see. It sounds confusing and frightening."

He could feel the tension in the car. He imagined he could feel her fury.

"You misunderstood me," she snapped.

"I don't think I did." Before she could argue, he pushed on. "The reason I don't think so is because when I was growing up my life was a little bit like that, and I didn't find it funny."

He had her attention. He felt her respond, and out of the corner of his eye he saw her move ever so slightly nearer to him.

"Yeah?" she asked in a soft voice.

"Yeah. I was a foster child and got moved around a lot from town to town, place to place. I didn't like it. I never felt like anybody really cared about me."

"Yeah?"

He could practically taste her interest. He had her, he was sure of it, and again he had the feeling that with this girl he'd better be a straight shooter. "I learned a lot of things too. One foster family loved baseball. I memorized all the Hall-of-Famers just to try and impress them."

"Did it?" She looked at him, wide-eyed.

"I don't know. I got moved a couple of days after I'd recited what I knew."

"Too bad."

He smiled. "Hey, I'm not trying to give you a sob story or anything. I just don't want you to try and kid me about how much fun this is for you. I know it's not much fun."

He heard her sigh deeply and glanced over at her in time to see her wipe her eyes. He thought she might have wiped away a tear, but he couldn't be sure.

"Now, you," he said. "You are definitely on the lucky side."

"How come?" she replied flippantly. "Because my mom marries guys with money?"

"Money has nothing to do with it. You have a family, and your family loves you."

"Like who?" She folded her arms across her chest.

"Like your Aunt Courtney and your grandmother. They've been worried sick about you."

"I don't ever even see them. I didn't think it would make a lot of difference to them."

"It did. Your Aunt Courtney has really suffered. She felt responsible for you."

"That's why she was worried, huh? Because she was supposed to be in charge. I heard my mom on the phone. She didn't even give Aunt Courtney a chance to say no."

"Did it ever cross your mind that maybe she didn't want a chance to refuse? She was thrilled to death."

"You're kidding."

"Why would I kid about it? She spent hours getting a room ready for you. She's missed school, she's in trouble with her boss for running off to Dallas to try to find you, but she never complained. She just wanted to have you with her."

Tracy looked at him guiltily. "I guess she's going to be good and mad at me, huh?"

"Wouldn't you say she has a right?"

Tracy didn't say anything.

"I'm not trying to be hard on you, kid. I like you. I'm only trying to point out what you've put your aunt through." His eyes left the highway long enough for him to gauge the effect of his words.

"You like me? Is that what you said?" she asked eagerly.

"Yeah, I do. I think you're cool."

She laughed hard, her voice high and melodic. "Nobody says cool anymore."

He felt as if he were old friends with this girl now that they'd talked. "Sorry about that. What's in?"

"Tough."

"Tough," he repeated. "Yeah, I think you're tough, all right." And he did.

"Thanks." She was obviously still pleased with herself. "So I'll apologize to Aunt Courtney. I already did once. I'll do it again."

"That will be good."

"Say, aren't you hungry yet? I could eat the tires off this car of yours."

He laughed and told her to choose a place for them to eat.

Everything seemed to be coming together, he thought as he turned off the highway in the direction of a fast-food restaurant. Tracy had been found. Courtney had said she loved him, and as soon as he could he would tell her he felt the same way about her. Something about sharing his feelings with this teenager had made him see that he'd been wrong, that he and Courtney both had been wrong.

He couldn't wait to tell her. He couldn't wait to hold Courtney in his arms.

Chapter Ten

Courtney answered the door before either Tracy or Mike had a chance to knock. She'd been listening for footsteps on the landing outside her apartment for the last hour.

"Tracy," she said when she saw the girl standing next to Mike. "Is it really you?" Courtney's eyes filled with tears. She put out her arms to greet her niece, and hugged her hard.

Tracy smiled at her aunt but didn't return her hug. Courtney drew back a little. "I'm so glad you're safe," she said, wiping away the tears that flooded her eyes.

"I—I want to apologize, Aunt Courtney. I'm sorry I caused you so much trouble." Tracy looked first at Courtney, then at Mike.

"Come in here," Courtney said, ushering them both into the apartment.

Mike brought Tracy's blaster, makeup bag and suitcase inside, and following Courtney's directions, carried them to the room that was to be Tracy's. When he came back into the living room the girl and her aunt were looking at one another in awkward silence.

"I'd better be going. I'll leave you two alone so you can get acquainted." He took Courtney's hand in his. "But I'll be back," he said, "tomorrow night so you and I can have a talk."

Oh, yes indeed, Courtney thought. Things would have to be settled between them once and for all. "Fine," she answered.

He let himself out, leaving the two of them alone. Courtney had not been herself, he thought as he headed wearily for his car.

She'd been chilly toward him, barely able to look directly at him. A wave of apprehension washed over him. He'd been trying to convince himself that nothing was wrong, but that wasn't true. He only hoped that tomorrow night they would be able to resolve whatever problems existed. He wanted time to think about what he was going to say to her, time to decide how he was going to explain himself to her.

Somehow, some way, he needed to find the words to seal their love forever.

After Mike had left them alone in the apartment, Tracy gave her aunt a nervous smile. "He said our eyes were the same. I hope so. You have pretty eyes."

"And you're beautiful," Courtney said, trying to make sense out of her emotions. Seeing Mike again had been unsettling. His physical presence was a reminder of how much she cared for him.

"Nice apartment," Tracy said, walking around the room.

Courtney watched the girl's movements. She was so much like her mother that it was amazing.

Tracy Blume was a lovely girl. She had the Evanses's rose-toned complexion and naturally wavy hair that had thousands of reddish highlights. Dressed in a pair of skintight jeans and a shirt two sizes too big, she still managed to have an air of sophistication about her that reminded Courtney of Chris. And so did the unhappy set of Tracy's beautiful face. Her eyes had no life. She was like Chris in so many ways.

"Are you hungry or anything?" Courtney asked, reminded by the look in Tracy's eyes that they'd both had a rough day.

"No, I'm on a diet."

"A diet?" Courtney laughed. "With your figure?"

Tracy eyed her. "You're not big on dieting? My mother sure is. She says if I get a pound over a hundred and seven I'm courting disaster."

Courtney grinned, ignoring the mental image she had of Chris telling her daughter she had to be perfect. "I think you look wonderful, and while you're here with me we won't discuss dieting. Let's put your things in your room and then have some cookies and ice cream. It's the best stuff you've ever put in your mouth, I guarantee."

"Fine, if you don't tell my mom."

Courtney gave her a conspiratorial grin and led her down the hall. The girl might be sophisticated for her age. She might be sixteen going on twenty-six, but nevertheless she was still a child. The look in her eyes when her mother's name was mentioned had been too obvious for anyone to miss.

"Here we are."

Tracy peered into the bedroom. "Is this where I'll be sleeping?" she asked.

"Yes. Do you like it?" Courtney knew it couldn't compare to her own room back home.

"Where do you sleep?" For the first time since she'd arrived, Tracy looked into Courtney's eyes. They stood in silence for a long moment.

"Right next door."

"It'll be great," she said, putting her blaster on top of the chest of drawers. Then she saw the kitten, which had come to see what all the commotion was about. She scooped it unceremoniously into her arms.

"What's his name?" Tracy asked, hugging the little ball of fur to her.

"*Her* name is Emily," Courtney said, and smiled.

"She's adorable. I love kittens.

"Why don't you and Emily get to know each other while I get the ice cream, okay?"

Tracy nodded, and Courtney went into the kitchen.

When she was searching through the freezer, she felt a presence behind her and whirled around. "Wha—."

"Sorry. I didn't mean to scare you." Tracy was watching her from the doorway.

"Oh, that's all right. I guess I'm not used to having anyone else around."

"Yeah. It's probably hard on you having someone barge in like this, isn't it? Especially after the stunt I pulled."

The girl's words washed away Courtney's discomfort. "Honey, it's no bother at all to have you. I'm thrilled to death that you're here with me."

"Even having to share your home with a stranger?"

"You're no stranger, Tracy Blume. Maybe we haven't seen one another as much as I'd like, but you're no stranger. I'm so happy to have you with me, I can't find the words to tell you how I feel."

"You are?" Tracy's question was tentative.

"Yes," Courtney exclaimed. "I'm absolutely thrilled. You don't know how many times I've begged Chris to come to see me or at least let you come."

"Really?" Tracy's blue eyes seemed brighter now.

"Really," Courtney insisted.

She took the girl in her arms. This time Tracy responded with an overpowering embrace of her own.

Thank you, God, Courtney said silently. *I've said the right thing. Thank you.*

"I've always wanted to get to know you," Tracy said then. Courtney went back to spooning the ice cream into bowls, and Tracy swung herself up to sit on the countertop across from her.

"Now it's my turn to be surprised. Why?"

"Because you have a nice smile. I've always remembered your smile, ever since I was a little girl."

Courtney laughed. "I have my mother's smile. Your grandmother smiles just like this." Courtney handed her her ice cream. "Come to think of it, your mouth is shaped like your grandmother's."

"I don't remember her much."

"No, you probably don't," Courtney said as the telephone rang.

"It's probably your mother or your grandmother calling to find out the latest," Courtney told her as she went to answer the phone.

"Hello."

Tracy had followed Courtney into the living room, eating her ice cream as she went.

After talking a few minutes, Courtney turned to Tracy, holding the telephone out to her. "It's your mother. She wants to talk to you."

Tracy's eyes grew large. She hesitated, confusion and regret on her face. "I..."

"She's worried about you."

Tracy put down her bowl of ice cream and took the receiver from Courtney. "He—hello," she said tentatively.

Courtney hurriedly left the room. It was important that Chris and Tracy talk privately.

A long time later, Tracy walked into Courtney's bedroom to find her aunt hard at work at her typewriter.

"Aunt Courtney, can we talk?"

"Sure," Courtney replied, motioning for her to have a seat on the bed. The second article in her series was progressing much better than the first, and she knew she'd get it in on time.

Tracy threw herself down on the bed. "You're not going to believe this," she said, laughter filling her voice.

"What?" Courtney left her desk and went to sit on the floor beside the bed, where she would be at eye level with Tracy.

"My mom says that when she comes home to Dallas, she's going to start seeing a therapist. She says she knows she needs someone to help her."

The exuberance in the girl's voice was contagious. "Oh, Tracy, that's wonderful," Courtney cried.

Tracy clapped her hands together. "You bet it is. See, Mom's never gotten help before."

"I know," Courtney answered.

"Well, don't you see? It could help her."

Courtney put out her hand and gently touched the girl's face. How had Chris been so lucky as to have this wonderful child? How had this child turned out to be so loving despite all the confusion in her life. Courtney's heart went out to her.

"Yes, it can. That's the best news we could have had."

"It sure is," Tracy said, nodding her head vigorously. "It really is. See, my mom just needs a little help. That's all."

"You love her, don't you?" Courtney said wistfully.

"Love my mom?" Tracy smiled. "She does some weird things but I love her a lot."

"And I love you," Courtney said, tears stinging her eyes.

Tracy stared up at the ceiling. "Sometimes—do you think it's possible that sometimes things that aren't right maybe work out for the best?" She glanced at Courtney, then turned her eyes back toward the ceiling. "I mean, my mom just said that my running off made her stop and think. She said it was like a thunderbolt had struck her. Does that make sense?"

"Yes." Courtney nodded. "It does."

Tracy curled over on her side and looked directly into Courtney's eyes. "I think I'm going to love you too, Aunt Courtney."

Those words stayed with Courtney. It had been like hearing the voice of an angel. And they helped her face her other problems.

When she'd been set free from her concerns for Tracy and was able to get a good night's sleep, she found her worries still weren't over. Throughout the night she dreamed of Mike. Each scene was different, yet the same. They were together, then apart. The settings were vastly different. The feelings were always identical.

Where, she wondered, had she lost her way? She'd promised herself over and over again that she would never develop an attachment for a man who wasn't open and expressive. She'd even gone so far as to fool herself into thinking she wasn't falling in love with Mike. Time and time again she'd mentally avoided the issue.

Now here she was, in love and hurting. And she had to tell him.

But what would be her reward if she were to be with him again—more pain? He had never really loved her, and she would be a complete and utter fool if she allowed him to stay in her life another moment. She'd been enough of a fool already. Nothing could change what she'd done. Now she had to decide how to face her future.

"When will the second article be ready?" Mr. Wagner demanded as soon as Courtney walked into the office the next morning.

"It's done," she said proudly. "I managed to finish it last night."

"Then come into my office right away, Miss Evans," he said, less belligerently than usual.

"I'll be right there."

She gathered up the article and her folder of notes. She'd be prepared for any questions he might ask, she told herself as she bolted down the hall, wiping the perspiration from her hands on her corduroy skirt. His burst of enthusiasm yesterday was so uncharacteristic that she was still feeling a little uneasy about it. He could change his mind at any minute. She'd seen her opinionated boss reverse himself frequently.

"Well, quick, let me see it," Mr. Wagner said the instant she entered his office. He was smoking a pipe, a habit he'd supposedly broken himself of several months before. He held his hand out to her impatiently.

"Here it is," she said, thrusting it at him.

Settling his glasses low on his nose, he read the article intently. After he'd finished, he looked up at her over the glasses.

"Well?" he said.

She didn't know what he wanted to hear. "Well," she answered.

"Do you like this one?"

She swallowed hard, then nodded. "Yes, sir." It was true. She did. The second article had been much easier to write than the first. In this one, she had told more about Mike the person. She had described his caring, his concern for both the innocent and the guilty. She thought she'd captured the essence of the true man.

"You should be." He puffed on his pipe. "Everybody who's seen your article so far has loved it. Personally, I think it's one of the best things we've published in years."

"*My* article?"

He glared at her. "Of course, *your* article, Courtney."

She caught the impatience in his voice, but at the same time she realized he'd called her by her first name. It was unbelievable.

"Oh, that's wonderful," she whispered.

"So wonderful that I've already set up space in Sunday's paper for you to interview this fellow about his reaction to your articles. You know, if these articles have as much impact as I think they'll have, the TV reporters will be all over him."

"I—" She hadn't thought about it, hadn't really considered the ways her articles would affect Mike's life.

"Anyway, let's get this one hopping, and you get out there and interview this fella tomorrow for Sunday's paper. I understand you brought your niece here with you today."

"Yes, sir."

"Glad things worked out for you," he said, and his expression changed to one of warmth.

"Thank you, sir."

"Get me a good interview for Sunday."

"Yes, sir," she answered, feeling vaguely uneasy. She didn't want to interview Mike again. She didn't want to see him any more than she had to. Tonight was going to be it. She'd say goodbye to him then.

She fixed Tracy her specialty, spaghetti and meatballs, when they got home that evening. As she listened to the girl describe her boyfriend and her life in Dallas, Courtney was thinking that she should be happy, ecstatically so. She had everything to be grateful for. She had her niece back in her life, and she had written two articles that had made her boss proud of her. A short while ago, she couldn't have dreamed of being so lucky.

But she was miserable. And it was all because she'd turned her rescuer into her lover, and had given her heart to him when he hadn't even wanted it.

After dinner, Tracy said she was tired but wanted to stay up until Mike got there. When he arrived later, Courtney watched the easy camaraderie between the two of them with more than a little surprise. Mike behaved as if he and Tracy were old friends, and although the girl had spoken of him kindly, Courtney hadn't been prepared for the close friendship that apparently existed between the two of them. It only served to make what she was about to do more difficult.

When Tracy had finally gone to bed, the two of them sat looking at one another across the small living room. Courtney was trying to decide how she wanted to begin the conversation, but Mike took the task away from her.

"Is something wrong? You seem nervous. I hope it's not because of the newspaper article. I'll admit I was surprised," he said with a grin, "but as I told Tracy before, flattered is mostly what I felt. I've had all sorts of people mention the article to me today. People seemed to like it."

From her seat on the sofa she stared at him. Mike had made himself comfortable in one of the rattan chairs.

His smile faded away and he assumed the brooding expression that had become so familiar to

Courtney. She'd tried to describe it in her articles, but felt that she'd failed to capture the alluring mystery of the man in a way that her readers could understand. One simply had to know Mike Harris.

"I've been wanting to talk to you about us, Courtney. I actually wanted to have this talk earlier, but I didn't have everything worked out." He moved to sit beside her on the sofa.

She pulled away from him almost imperceptibly. "I've been wanting to talk to you too, Mike."

"I know, I know," he said, nodding his head and smiling at her. "Things have happened so fast between us. I'm sure you feel it, too. Who'd have dreamed?" He tried to take her hand in his, but instead she clasped her hands in her lap.

"You're right," she said. "Who would have dreamed?"

"Courtney, for days I've been trying to think of the best way to approach this subject with you. I guess it's been in the back of my mind for some time. It took your niece to bring things into focus for me, and I'll always be grateful to her for that."

"Tracy?" She didn't understand what he meant, but his movements, and the looks he was giving her, were making her uncomfortable.

He was sitting too close. She could see too much in those dark, perceptive eyes of his. He was so near that she imagined she could feel his energy, his heat, his aura of masculinity.

Courtney felt her resolve waver, and knew that she had to speak. "I'm grateful for your help, Mike. I'm sure you know that. But now—"

"But now that all your problems are behind you," he interrupted, "it's time to concentrate on us. Something happened to me, Courtney, when I talked to Tracy on the way back from Dallas. I realized that we, the two of us, were behaving like intimate strangers. That's all Tracy's ever known for step-fathers—intimate strangers. I've been trying to live my life that way, too, going around, calling what I do living and doing everything I can not to get emotionally involved with anyone. I didn't want to care about another person. I'd locked myself away. I didn't want to love you, Courtney. I tried my best not to. But I did. I started falling in love with you the day I first met you. When you spoke of love to me the other night—" he took her hand in his, resisting her slight effort to pull free "—I was too choked up to tell you I loved you. I couldn't get the words out."

Courtney was staring at him. She was totally unprepared for what she was hearing. His firm voice was as smooth as honey, as compelling as a magical spell.

But she had to resist him. "I shouldn't have said that to you," she said flatly. She shook her head. "It was a mistake."

"It wasn't a mistake. It was wonderful. It was the most wonderful thing I've ever heard. I was the one who was wrong. I was the one who couldn't tell you what I felt."

He tried to take her into his arms, but her back stiffened and as she pulled away he found himself reaching for empty air. He saw the pain in her eyes, and his heart told him things were very wrong between them. It seemed his declaration of love had fallen on deaf ears.

"It was a mistake," she insisted.

"Courtney, I love you. That's no mistake."

She started to protest, but Mike rushed on. "Look, I'm trying to say this the right way. I don't remember ever telling anyone I loved her. Ever. Not even my wife. It's hard for me to explain this." He shook his head. "No. Hard isn't the right word. It's not hard. It's easy to tell you because I want you to know, but it's unfamiliar." He smiled at her.

His smile was devastating, and she pulled her gaze away from his face. Looking at him was painful.

"Mike, I don't think you know what you're saying. I think you're on a follow-up mission, just like the ones you conduct on your job, just like the one you did with me before." Tears threatened her, but she managed to hold them back while she talked. "I think you went with me to Dallas because it was your way of being kind to a friend. Originally you said you wanted to be friends. Proving to be a good one meant accompanying me, especially when you saw that I was falling apart with worry over Tracy. And then, things just happened. I needed you. I needed your warmth and your affection. I wanted to go to bed with you. I needed you, and you were searching for some way to comfort me. You did it in the most intimate way you knew how."

"Courtney, that's a—"

"Please don't interrupt me," she begged. "From the beginning, you've made no bones about it, Mike. You didn't want involvement. You became much more involved with me and my problems than you ever intended. I know that. I worried about it all the way to Dallas, and even afterward. I've been aware of it all along. I was the one who pulled you into all of this, and it's my fault that I fell in love with you. You owe me nothing." A wayward tear glistened on her dark eyelash. "But now I . . . I don't want to see you anymore. Seeing you is too painful a reminder of the fool I've been."

"Oh, no, Courtney," he cried, taking her in his arms. "You're wrong."

She pushed him back, freeing herself instantly. His arms promised comfort and tenderness. The smell of his skin was wonderfully familiar, his touch enticing. She knew if she let him hold her she'd succumb. She'd crumble and fall into his arms, throw away her last shred of self-respect.

She stood up and took several steps away from Mike. "Don't tell me I'm wrong. I don't want to hear it."

"Courtney, what can I do? I'm trying to tell you what's in my heart."

"Oh, Mike," she whispered, "don't you see? Maybe you think you love me, but you don't. You've just been going with the flow, and now you want to make things right for me. It's my fault, not yours. *I* fell in love with *you*. I brought all this on myself."

"Courtney, I'm in love with you. Nothing you do or say will make me change my mind."

"Go away, Mike." She began to cry now, unable to choke back the burning tears. "Just do me a favor and go away."

He stood up. "I'll go, but I'll be back."

"No," she answered. "It would be better if you didn't."

He stormed to the door, then turned back to face her. "I don't understand why you won't allow yourself to hear me, but I'm not going to give up. No matter what you want, I'll be back."

He threw the door open and left her standing there, alone and aching. She couldn't allow herself to see him again. Next time she might not be as strong as she had been tonight. And she knew she had to be.

She couldn't handle any more pain. She had had enough.

Chapter Eleven

Aunt Courtney, you look tired," Tracy said, when they were having breakfast the next morning. "Didn't you get any sleep last night, or did Mike stay too long?" She took a last sip of her orange juice and stretched her arms high above her head. "I was so tired, I fell asleep the second my head hit the pillow."

Courtney rubbed her face. She knew she looked bad. Two dark splotches had settled directly underneath her tired eyes, and her skin was pale.

"I didn't sleep very well. Maybe I was too tired."

"Maybe you were just excited." Tracy grinned. "About today and all."

Courtney tried to return the girl's smile. "Well," she said, making an effort to get her mind back on track, "I certainly have a lot to be excited about, don't I?"

"Don't *we*, you mean." Tracy tried to drink orange juice from the glass she'd already drained.

"Do you want some more, dear? It's in the pitcher on the counter." Courtney watched her spring up from her chair and wished the girl could transfer some of that boundless energy to her aunt. Depressed and still upset from the night before, Courtney felt as if a heavy cloud had settled over her and would never leave.

"I mean," Tracy went on, "what with my grandmother coming today and my mother coming in tomorrow, it's going to be like Grand Central Station around here, isn't it?"

"Probably." Courtney tried to pull her attention away from herself. "You act as though you're anxious to see your grandmother."

"I am," Tracy answered. "Want some more juice?" She held up the pitcher.

"No, thanks."

"Coffee?" She headed toward the kettle on the stove.

"No, thanks. I've had two cups. That's my limit."

Courtney watched Tracy as she sat back down. It was amazing, she thought, that this niece of hers had turned out to be such a generous, caring person. She couldn't wait for Alma Evans to spend the weekend with this girl. She'd be thrilled with her granddaughter.

"Say, do you think we should cook for them?"

"I think we should," Courtney said, wondering where she'd find the strength.

"Maybe tonight, though, we could take grandmother out to eat. If you're going to work all day, you'll probably be tired tonight."

"Now look at me. Do I look tired to you?" Courtney said teasingly.

With a laugh, Tracy stood up and started clearing the dishes off the table. "You're very pretty, Aunt Courtney. Even when you look tired."

"When you grow up you should think about becoming a politician."

"Good line, huh?"

"Right."

Courtney headed back to her room to dress for work. They had agreed that Courtney would go to work today and Tracy would remain in the apartment and await her grandmother. Mrs. Evans had said she'd arrive around twelve, but Courtney assured Tracy that she'd probably be there much earlier. Tracy had seemed excited about the prospect of spending a few hours alone with her grandmother.

When Courtney was dressed and making up her bed, Tracy came into her bedroom. "You don't mind, do you?"

"Mind what?"

"My coming in."

Courtney went over to Tracy, gave her a hasty kiss on the forehead and then went around to the other side of the bed. "Are you kidding? I love it."

Tracy plopped down on the room's one chair. "You know," she said, "I'd like my boyfriend a whole lot better if he was something like Mike." She stared out the window. "I mean, Mike is just about the nicest guy I ever met. His life hasn't been too easy, you know, what with not having any family, and then marrying a woman who was pregnant with someone else's child."

"Actually," Courtney said, trying not to gasp at the revelation, "I don't know a great deal about his life."

"I do," Tracy said nonchalantly.

Courtney looked at her. "You do?" Well, she thought, it certainly seemed that the girl did. She knew more than Courtney, anyway.

"Yeah. We talked for the entire four-and-a-half hours it took to drive to San Antonio. He told me everything himself. We've got a lot in common, Mike and I."

Courtney found herself holding the bedspread purposelessly up in the air. Her mind was going over and over what Tracy was saying.

Mike had cared enough to reveal a great deal of his personal history to a sixteen-year-old child whom he'd never met before. Had he done it in the interest of helping Tracy, or had he done it because the girl had touched him in some way. Courtney realized she might never know the answer.

She dropped the bedspread, and in two quick moves, finished her chore. Still in shock at what she'd heard, she grabbed her jacket from the open closet and slipped it on.

"I'm going to be late if I don't hurry, sweetie. Are you sure you'll be all right staying here by yourself?"

"Sure," Tracy promised, jumping up to walk her to the door. "I'll be fine. If something happens I can call Mike. He gave me his phone number." She smiled at Courtney. "But don't worry. I'll watch television till grandmother gets here, and I'll call you when she shows up."

Courtney left the apartment and hurried to her car. She felt guilty, but she was glad to be getting away. Hearing Tracy recite details about Mike that she didn't know, and hearing of the closeness the girl felt for him, was more than Courtney could handle right now.

She was too confused. She hadn't begun to recover from last night, when he'd proclaimed his love for her. It had caught her completely off guard.

She'd wanted to hear him out. She'd wanted to give in, but she hadn't been able to give herself permission.

If he really did love her, why hadn't he said so before? Why had he allowed her to voice her feelings, and then answer her with "Let me hold you"?

If what he'd said was true, if he'd really been unable to express what he felt, then he wasn't what she wanted in the first place, was he? Hadn't she sworn off men who couldn't say what they felt?

What kind of generous man was he that he'd married someone who was pregnant with another man's child? Was he giving the baby a name? Had family and name meant that much to him? And if he had married once out of compassion more than love, didn't that make his declaration of love to her even more suspect?

Her head was pounding as she drove into the parking lot at work. She didn't want to think anymore. She wanted to forget. She'd be so much better off if she could only forget the way he'd made love to her, the way he'd held her, the way his lips had felt as they'd claimed hers.

"No," she said aloud as she got out of the car and headed for her office. "That's enough." She marched into the office, intent upon concentrating on her work and nothing else.

"The phone calls just keep pouring in," Mary Claire told her when she got to her desk. "The boss says you're doing a special piece for the front page of Sunday's paper."

The color drained from Courtney's face. Damn it all, she'd forgotten about the article. How could she do it? She'd vowed last night not to see him again.

"Earth to Mars, are you there?" Mary Claire teased.

"Yes," Courtney answered. "I'm here." A thought struck her then. "Mary Claire, why don't you do this article? You talk to Mike Harris about his reaction to having been written up in the newspaper."

Mary Claire glared at her. "Have you lost your mind, friend? I do obits and weddings. That's all. Besides, I don't think Mr. Wagner would like it one little bit. He wants you to do it. He's going to use your picture on the front page. Osgood told me."

"How are you and Osgood doing? Any progress?"

"Slow but sure, now that he's convinced you're in love with the policeman."

Courtney stared up at her friend. "What?"

"Osgood says he can sense it. Your eyes are bright and you smile a lot to yourself or you stare off into space. Osgood says that's a true sign of love."

"Mary Claire, I've only been back in the office two days."

Courtney's friend shrugged and grinned wickedly. "Can I help it if Osgood thinks he knows something? Whether it's right or wrong, I want him to go on thinking it." Mary Claire turned and walked away, leaving Courtney alone with her thoughts.

The intercom on her desk buzzed. "Miss Evans, is your piece ready for Sunday?" Mr. Wagner's voice boomed through the wire.

"Uh, no sir, it's not."

"When will you have it?" he asked impatiently.

"Soon."

"How soon is soon?" He refused to let her off the hook.

"Uh, Detective Harris is on duty and can't be disturbed. I'll try to get it first thing tomorrow."

"Drop it by my house. I'll be on the golf course tomorrow, but I want to see it before it goes into print. See that it's there before twelve, and someone will get it to me." He clicked off the intercom without signing off.

Then she heard it buzz again. "Yes?"

"By the way, this thing you're doing is having phenomenal success. I've had calls from the television stations. Don't be surprised if they try to contact you." He chuckled. "Who knows? This might make you a media star."

"Yes, sir," she whispered, thinking she still wasn't certain she'd be able to conduct the interview.

She spent the rest of the day in torment over the prospect of seeing Mike again to do the interview. Her only relief was hearing from Tracy. She called to report on her grandmother's arrival, and her voice sounded so rich and full of life that it perked up Courtney's spirits just to talk to her.

As soon as she could leave work, Courtney raced home. "Hi," she cried when she hit the front door.

"Shh," Tracy said, pressing a finger to her lips. "Grandmother's asleep."

"Oh." Softly Courtney closed the door behind her. "How'd the day go?"

"The day went super," Tracy exclaimed in a stage whisper. "Come on into the kitchen and I'll give you a chocolate-chip cookie. Grandmother's secret recipe."

Courtney wasn't about to tell Tracy that she knew for a fact that her mother had always used the recipe on the back of the chocolate chip packages.

"How often do you go to visit grandmother?" Tracy asked when she'd given Courtney a stack of cookies and a glass of milk. They sat at the kitchen counter.

"Oh, I don't know. Not often enough. Why?" Courtney watched the girl's face.

"Nothing. Just wondering if my mom would let me go."

"I'm sure she would, Tracy. You're old enough to travel by yourself now. You've done it already," she teased.

"Yeah, you're right."

Courtney studied the girl's face. "Tracy, if your grandmother thought you'd want to visit her in Austin, she'd move heaven and earth to make it happen. She loves you."

"Loves me? She hardly knows me," Tracy said wistfully.

"Of course she loves you."

"Why?" Tracy put down her cookie.

"Because you're her granddaughter. That's the first thing."

"My mother says love is not an obligation. It has to be earned."

Courtney swallowed a mouthful of milk before she answered, praying her words would be the right ones.

"I don't agree. I believe love is unconditional. We're blood relatives, and we love one another because we're family." She paused. "You're family, Tracy. No matter what. Your grandmother loves you. I love you. All your other aunts and uncles love you. We want the chance to know you better, to be real friends, real family." She stopped and took a deep breath. "But even if we don't get that chance, which I'm hoping we will, we're still going to love you."

"Real family," Tracy said with a distant look in her eyes. "That's what Mike said he'd always wanted, a real family." She shook her head. "I guess he's right. I'm lucky. I've got one."

Unmindful of the glass she knocked over, Courtney suddenly threw her arms around Tracy. She had to blink back tears, tears of joy over finding Tracy and having her in her life, and tears of sorrow over Mike and the loss she was feeling.

When the telephone rang, Tracy raced to answer it. She came back into the kitchen. "For you," she said, and grabbed another cookie.

"Hello," Courtney said, and listened as a fast-talking TV newswoman introduced herself and then proceeded to explain why she'd called.

One of the local stations wanted to conduct a dual interview with Courtney and Mike. They'd set it up, the woman said, for the early-evening Saturday news report.

"You mean we'd be doing this at the same time?" Courtney asked, "I mean, together?"

"Why, yes."

"I don't think so," she told the woman.

"Look, we've moved heaven and earth to get Detective Harris to agree to this. Surely, as a fellow reporter, you wouldn't mind getting a little exposure yourself. Think of how it will help your paper's sales, not to mention your career."

"I'm sorry I'd just rather not do it," she said, and hung up. She closed her eyes and rubbed her forehead, trying to ease the tension.

Cutting off her nose to spite her face. That's what her mother would say she was doing. A chance to be interviewed on television was something few reporters would refuse. Giving it up was foolish. But she couldn't be near Mike. Not now. She wasn't strong enough.

The doorbell rang, and her mother came out of the bedroom at the same time. "Tracy, could you get that?" Courtney called, greeting her mother with a hug. "Hi."

"Hi yourself," her mother said. "Let me look at you. I haven't seen you in a long time either." Pulling herself up to her full five-foot-two, Mrs. Evans said, "Why is it that you look so tired and that beautiful granddaughter of mine looks so rested? You need more rouge. You're too pale."

"Thanks, Mom," Courtney answered with a laugh.

"I can't help it. The mother in me gets in the way. How are you, darling?"

"Fine. I'm just fine," she lied.

Courtney escorted her mother into the living room. Curious to know who Tracy was talking to, she strained her ears to hear, but no voices were loud enough for her to make out anything. She could only hope it wasn't a TV reporter or someone like that come to pester her.

"Hello, Courtney," Mike said, following Tracy into the living room.

Courtney gasped and inadvertently took a step backward. He couldn't be here, she thought. How could she possibly bear to see him now? But even as she stared at him, her heart leaped, hungry for the sound of his voice, the sight of his commanding figure. Despite herself, she'd missed him. She'd missed him too much.

"Grandmother, this is the man I told you about," Tracy announced with a big smile. "This is Mike."

Mrs. Evans put out her hand and Mike took it. "Hello. I've been looking forward to meeting you," he said with the diplomacy of a master politician and the disarming grin that had so captivated Courtney's heart.

Courtney's mother was smiling too. "And I'm very happy to meet you, Mike. For all the things you've done for us, I want to express our family's gratitude." She put her arm around Tracy. "I'm very glad my granddaughter chose to have her little rebellion when you were around to help Courtney and the rest of us through it."

Courtney watched Mike and her mother. They seemed comfortable with one another. As they sat and continued their conversation, all three of them seemed at ease. And, although by now she'd thought she'd had enough surprises, Courtney couldn't help but find it fascinating that her mother had obviously banished all reservations about Mike from her mind.

"Courtney was quite capable of handling this on her own," Mike was saying. "I went along because I wanted to, not because she needed me."

"Oh, that's not at all—" She stopped herself, unwilling to be drawn into a conversation in which she and Mike spent their time praising one another. She lowered her gaze away from his intense stare and felt her cheeks flush with color.

Damn, damn, damn, how could he have come like this? How could he make himself at home and behave as though he belonged there? And how could her family be so receptive to him, welcoming him like a long-lost relative?

She grew silent while the three of them talked. From the conversation, it was evident that Tracy had already told her grandmother what she'd done and why. Now Courtney's mother and Mike were discussing teenage rebellion and the forms it could take. Every now and then Tracy would say something, but the conversation was very much between Mike and Courtney's mother.

Courtney still couldn't get over the way her mother was behaving. She was making everything Courtney had told Mike about the family opinion of policemen seem a lie. She was smiling and winking at him, and every now and then she tapped him on the knee when she wanted to make an important point. The entire situation made no sense at all to Courtney.

When Courtney was finally able to get her mind off herself for a moment, she heard her mother say, "We were thinking of going to a place Tracy said you had recommended, Mike. The Lone Star Cafe."

"Yes. The food's good. Chicken-fried steak is the house specialty." He was looking at Courtney when he spoke.

"We haven't even asked Courtney yet if she wanted to go out to eat, but it sounded like a fun spot," Mrs. Evans said.

Mike saw Courtney's look of apprehension and knew she was afraid he'd go with them.

What had happened? he wondered.

He'd thought he was giving her everything and he had demanded nothing. He'd offered her friendship. He'd tried to show that he cared.

But what it had all finally boiled down to was his silence. When she'd said she loved him, he'd choked, gone utterly silent.

And his silence had cost him Courtney. She was lost to him now. But he loved her deeply. It had taken him a while to realize it and forever to express it, but it was because he had spent too much of his life trying to protect himself from getting hurt. He didn't really know how to demonstrate affection and tenderness, although he had tried his best to do so since he'd met Courtney. For a man like himself, he'd thought it had been an outstanding job.

He watched her face, trying to decide what to do. How could he make her understand that he loved her?

"I have an idea," Tracy said. "Why don't you go with us, Mike?"

"I'm sure Detective Harris has better things to—"

He stopped Courtney in midsentence. "I have a suggestion for the two of you. Courtney and I have to talk. Why don't you go on down to the Lone Star Cafe and she can join you later? I'll tell you where it is."

Courtney was fuming and tried to protest, but before she could say anything Mike began to give directions to the restaurant. He wouldn't let her get a word in edgewise until Tracy and Courtney's mother had gone.

When they were alone, Mike looked across the room at Courtney. "I had to talk to you," he told her, seeing the rage in her pale blue eyes.

"But there's no point in talking. I told you that last night," she said, leaving the room.

He followed her, but she fled into her bedroom and slammed the door shut behind her.

"I'm not leaving without talking to you," he said through the closed door.

"Well, I'm not listening." Despite herself, she stood right by the door. She wanted to hear what he had to say. She wanted to find out if the man was actually able to speak of his emotions and his feelings.

"You know, it's funny," he was saying. "Your mother seems much more sensible than—than I had her pictured. She liked me. I could tell. I liked her, too."

He waited, but she said nothing. "I think it's funny that you held me off for so long because you said your family hated policemen."

Was he calling her a liar? "It was true," she argued.

"Well, if it was true, I certainly had an easy time breaking down the barriers."

"Because Tracy's life could have been at stake. That's why. You helped me. I've admitted that. I told you I was grateful."

He had her talking now, and he wasn't about to let up on her. "I like Tracy. She likes me, too."

"Yeah. You're a big hit with the family."

"All except you. Somehow I've managed to strike out with you."

"Mike, please," she begged him. "Please let this thing die."

"Die? I can't let it die," he shouted angrily. "My God, woman, what kind of feelings do you have that you could say 'I love you' and then turn around and tell me to let this thing between us die? You may find that it makes sense to you, but I don't. My feelings can't be shut off so easily."

"So easily," she cried, suddenly flinging the bedroom door open and facing him. "How can you say that? I told you what agony this was for me."

"Well, I'm trying to stop the agony for both of us."

"Look." She put her hand up in a gesture of warning. "I told you yesterday that I accepted the blame for trying to change things between us. I don't know what happened to me." She shook her head, still amazed at herself. "I was the one who tried to change the ground rules."

"What's wrong with changing your mind?" he demanded in exasperation. "You did. I did. We both did. And it's great."

"No, Mike." She shook her head vehemently. "You didn't. What you're saying now is in response to what happened in Dallas. That's all it is."

Unable to handle his frustration, he pounded the door with his fist. "You won't believe me because I didn't say 'I love you' to you that night? Because I waited," he cried. "I explained all that, damn it."

"I know," she said without conviction.

"No, you don't know. You can't know what I'm feeling, what I'm thinking. I don't know where you got the idea that it was okay for you to change your mind about us, but if I did, it wouldn't count."

Courtney felt hot and cold at the same time. She was afraid she might weaken at any moment. She felt as if he could read her thoughts, felt as if he knew what she was truly feeling. "It makes no difference now. Please go, Mike," she begged.

"Damn it, Courtney. Don't say that. Of course it makes a difference. Everything that goes on between us makes a difference."

She shook her head, trying to clear the cobwebs from her mind. The room felt hot and stuffy.

"No," she whispered.

"I'm tired of hearing you say no." He drew in his breath and paused.

"I had a revelation when I was with Tracy. That's the only way I know to describe it. Before, like I said, I'd made up my mind that I loved you. But when she and I were talking I decided I'd been wrong in the first place. I told you I wanted no commitments, no ties. Now I know that that was selfish and pigheaded, and if you'd had any sense then you'd have kicked me out of your apartment the night I so pompously declared what kind of relationship I wanted. Now I realize that without commitment this relationship of ours is like a flower with no roots, a lovely flower destined for an early death. I don't want that." He was shaking his head. "I don't want that to happen to us."

He tried to take her in his arms, but she refused, retreating toward the living room. He dropped his hands to his sides and leaned his head against the wall.

Finally, in a voice choked with emotion, he said, "I don't understand how you can dislike me so and write the things about me that you're writing. You're making me out to be some kind of hero, but to you I'm nothing. Well, let me tell you something. All my life I've looked for love, and now that I've found it it hurts worse than being alone."

When she didn't say anything he slowly made his way to the front door. "I love you, Courtney. I need you."

His voice was quiet, but it seemed to echo through the apartment long after he was gone.

His words reverberated through her mind. She felt cold and numb.

How could love hurt so much, he'd asked, and she'd had no answer. She still felt dizzy and disoriented.

The man had said he loved her. He had expressed his innermost feelings far better than she had ever done. He'd opened his mouth, given voice to his emotions and sealed her heart to his.

When she'd heard him speak so eloquently of his love for her, she'd been speechless, the dizziness leaving her mute, the words filling her senses. And now he was gone.

"Mike," Courtney called when she found her voice, but her only answer was silence. "Oh, Mike," she cried and ran to the window in time to see his shadow moving away from her in the night.

Chapter Twelve

For the rest of the evening Courtney did her best to keep her mother and Tracy from finding out how distraught she was. When she was able to, she went to the telephone as discreetly as possible and called Mike's home, but there was never an answer.

She couldn't escape the feelings that were assaulting her. When Mike had finally been able to give voice to his emotions, she'd let him down. She'd held back what was in her heart just as she'd accused him of having done for so long.

Now she wondered if it was too late for them. Mike wasn't the sort of man who'd give away his heart and then stand by and wait. By now he was probably furious at her. Perhaps he'd never want to speak to her again.

As she laughed and joked with Tracy and her mother, secretly feeling nothing but pain and remorse, she tried to think. Was it over? Had she lost Mike's love forever?

No, she thought, but tears sprang to her eyes. He did love her. He'd said so.

"Courtney, are you all right?" her mother asked.

Courtney brushed the tears away. "Sure," she said, "it's just that it's hard to believe we're all together."

Her mother beamed. "You're making me weepy, too," she said. "Time for a little hot chocolate." She turned to Tracy. "Come on, dear, if you want to learn how to make the best hot cocoa this side of the Mississippi."

Courtney smiled after they'd gone into the kitchen. Another of her mother's famous recipes. Straight off the cocoa box.

The telephone rang, and Courtney glanced down at her watch. Ten-thirty was a little late for someone to call, she thought.

"Hello."

"Miss Evans? It's Kitty Hall from WBXT again. Just wanted to check with you. We're all set for our interview with Detective Harris tomorrow. We'd like to extend the invitation to you once again. I think it would be great publicity for you, and I wish you'd reconsider."

"Oh, I don't think so, Miss Hall, but thanks," Courtney said listlessly.

"I can't believe you'd pass up this opportunity. When I talked to him earlier, Detective Harris specifically asked if you'd be there."

"He did?" It dawned on her then that perhaps this was her chance. She wanted to talk to Mike. The television interview would give her the opportunity. "What time did you say you wanted me there?" she asked, already making her plans for tomorrow.

The next morning, after a hearty breakfast, Courtney took Tracy and her mother for a tour of San Antonio, hitting all the important places—the Alamo, the Lone Star Pavilion, the Mexican market and the Riverwalk.

Now that she'd decided to see Mike, she felt much better, and she was able to give her attention to her family. Tracy was excited because she was looking forward to her mother coming home. Courtney's mother had her granddaughter and was ecstatic. She and Tracy were eagerly making plans for their next reunion.

When they returned from their excursion there was a message on Courtney's answering machine from Mr. Wagner. "I'm waiting for your front-page interview." His voice crackled over the hum of the machine.

"Tracy, Mom, you two will excuse me for a few minutes, won't you? I've got to write out a piece for the paper that's overdue."

"Sure, dear, we'll just go in and fix ourselves a little snack. Let's see, Tracy, what other old family recipes can I introduce you to?" Mrs. Evans said as she led Tracy to the kitchen.

Courtney had two hours before she was due at the television station. She hadn't done anything about her front-page interview. Somehow it had ceased to seem important. In fact, even her job didn't seem very important anymore.

She sat at her typewriter, trying to come up with something, anything. Finally she held her breath and wrote. It was a gamble. A desperate gamble. But she'd try it, she told herself, smiling as she did so.

Later, when she'd fixed her hair, applied her makeup slightly more heavily than usual and dressed in a peacock-blue dress and matching shoes, she said goodbye to Tracy and her mother, warning them that she might be late returning.

She drove to the studio, her anxiety mounting with each passing moment. Would this work? Could she convince Mike that she'd finally heard him, really heard him, and that she loved him? She had to. She had no other choice.

At the studio Courtney saw his car parked outside, and her heart leaped. Taking several deep breaths before going in, she tried to calm herself, but her attempts were not doing any good.

She was greeted at the door by one of the staff and immediately led into Makeup, but the makeup man said she had done a great job all on her own. Without so much as touching her, he banished Courtney to the waiting room.

Mike was nowhere to be seen, and she was grateful for that. Trying to regain her perspective before she got in front of the television cameras, Courtney realized she hadn't anticipated how nervous she'd be at the prospect of seeing him again. She shut her eyes and counted to ten. Then Courtney walked toward a woman she assumed was Kitty Hall.

"Miss Hall," Courtney said when she reached her side. "I'm Courtney Evans." She tried to smile, but couldn't quite manage it.

"Hello, Miss Evans. Thank you for coming." The blond reporter was dressed immaculately in a bright purple suit. She gave Courtney a firm handshake. "Detective Harris is on the phone. He'll join us in a moment. Have a seat, please, and our people will start preparing your microphone."

Courtney did as she was instructed. Someone clipped a microphone to her dress and talked into it for her, making the necessary adjustments. The lights overhead were hot and so bright that they put everything except the immediate setting in dark shadows.

Unable to see anyone, she sat alone, waiting for Mike.

She was thinking hard, suddenly on the verge of panic. What if this didn't work? What if Mike was so angry at her he didn't care what she said or did?

"Here we go, Miss Evans." Kitty Hall sat down next to Courtney and an attendant fastened a microphone to the lapel of her suit. "Josh, make sure we get Harris in here in time for his microphone check," she cautioned one of her assistants.

The minutes ticked by, and still Mike didn't appear. The studio was a flurry of activity as Kitty Hall dispatched one person after another to find him.

"We're on countdown," Kitty Hall said. "Somebody find him." There was an edge of panic in her voice.

Suddenly a camera zoomed in on the woman, its red light flashing. "Good evening," she said in a voice like silk. "I'm Kitty Hall. Welcome to WBXT and *Focus on San Antonio*. This afternoon's guests are Courtney Evans, reporter for the *San Antonio Light*, and—" She paused.

At last Mike joined them. Courtney watched as his microphone was attached to the lapel of his gray pinstriped suit. He wore a white shirt and a red silk tie. It was the first time she'd seen him so well dressed, and he'd never looked more handsome. The lines around his mouth were more relaxed than usual. He looked at the announcer, but not at Courtney.

"And to my left is Detective Mike Harris, who has come into local prominence through a series of articles written by Miss Evans."

Mike smiled warmly into the camera.

"First you, Miss Evans. I'd like to know what made you focus on a police negotiator."

Courtney's eyes went to Mike, but he refused to return her look. Nervously she answered, "I, uh, I . . . I decided that not many of us knew what services we had in our city, and a police negotiator, I felt, would be someone of interest to all our citizens. As I got to know more about Detective Harris and how devoted he was to his work, I felt he'd make the perfect personal-interest entry for my series on police work."

"And what about the personal side of this, Miss Evans? If my information is correct, Detective Harris actually saved your life." The camera was moving from Courtney to Mike and back again.

"Yes," she said, then swallowed. She hadn't anticipated telling this part. It hadn't been in her articles. "That's true." She went on to describe the incident, reliving it as she did so.

"So that's how you came to identify him as 'The Rescuer.' Wasn't that what you wrote in your article? I believe you called him 'The Rescuer.'"

"Yes. He is." Courtney smiled then. "He certainly was for me, in more ways than one." When

Mike glanced at her sharply she met his look, hoping she could convey what she was feeling.

"And Detective Harris, how do you feel about the title?"

His dark eyes didn't waver from Courtney's face. "I think Miss Evans deserves the title more than I do," he declared. "I rescued her in the line of duty. She rescued me in another way."

The announcer frowned. "What do you mean, Detective Harris?"

Courtney heard him speak, and her heart lifted with his words.

"One of the drawbacks to what I do is the emotional strain it creates. Most policemen end up keeping a lot inside. Miss Evans has taught me the importance of expressing emotions."

"Oh, really," the newswoman said. From her tone of voice, it was evident that she was trying to regain her bearings. She'd lost the focus on her own show, and now it was up to her to recapture what she'd lost.

Kitty Hall smiled into the camera. "We'll be right back with more of our interview after these words." As soon as the camera light had flashed off, she turned to her assistant. "How're we doing? Should we pick back up on the police negotiator aspect or concentrate on the two of them?" It seemed not to occur to her to talk to Mike and Courtney about where the interview was going. She was concerned with ratings, and with how her show came across to the viewers.

"I have something I want you to read," Courtney whispered to Mike while Kitty Hall made her decision. She took a piece of paper from her purse. "It's a news brief I'm supposed to have handed in this morning. If you approve, I'll rush it to the paper right after we finish here."

There was a long pause, and he stared straight into her eyes for several seconds. When he spoke it was with reluctance. "I don't want to talk business with you, Courtney. It's bad enough having to be here, sitting across from you, seeing you like this. But at least I'm saying what I feel. And I like doing it, even though I'm probably making a fool of myself."

"Just read this. Please." She pressed the paper into his hand.

"We're on the air," Kitty Hall said, as she turned back to face the camera. She turned to Mike. "Detective Harris, a few moments ago you were speaking of your inability to express your emotions. I want to tell the viewers a little bit about what your job consists of and then I want to come back to what you said."

She glanced down at the clipboard she held. "First, viewers, I want to tell you that it was no easy feat getting the facts I'm about to relate to you. Detective Harris is a reluctant hero. He has requested that his record not be made public, but we felt it was important that you know." She gave Mike a quick smile, then looked intently into the camera. "Mike Harris referred to his job as stressful. Let me tell you why." She paused dramatically. "He breaks up family disturbances. He rescues children from the hands of people who are trying to harm them. He talks people out of committing suicide. He meets death and violence at every turn. In one single day he might work with as many as five people whose lives are in danger. That's what he does for a living. That's what he does for you." Her eyes caressed the camera. "For all of us."

She waited a few moments for that to sink in with the viewers at home. She swung her body around to face Mike, and the camera followed suit. "Tell me about emotions," she said, and the camera zoomed in, focusing on his face.

Courtney was amazed at the way Kitty Hall was able to build up the drama and intensity of the interview. The woman was definitely good at what she did. She staged everything to grab the public interest.

Looking from Kitty to Mike, Courtney gasped and then smiled broadly. The interview suddenly seemed inconsequential; all her nervousness vanished. Mike returned her smile, a look of love and happiness on his face. He had read the piece of paper she'd handed him. His entire body leaned forward, giving the impression that at any moment he might jump up and come to her. Courtney was ecstatic. His response had been more than she could have asked for.

"Detective Harris," the interviewer was saying. "What about your emotions?"

Finally he looked at her, but he wasn't really looking. He was thinking about Courtney, about the two of them, about what the future might hold for them.

"I am very much in contact with my emotions," he said. "At one time I considered giving up my job. Now I realize that I love it, and I intend to stay with it."

Courtney smiled. All along she'd secretly hoped he wouldn't give up what she knew he did so well.

"Detective Harris, we only have a few moments more. Can you tell our viewers what this publicity has done for you?" Kitty Hall was ready to cap off the program. She waited for him to speak.

He looked at Courtney and grinned. "Maybe I can tell you by reading this to you. It will be in the paper soon."

"Very well," the newswoman said, nervously tightening her grip on her clipboard.

"Detective Mike Harris and Courtney Evans, reporter for the *San Antonio Light*, announce their engagement. Although no date has been set for the wedding, the couple confirms that the nuptials will take place as soon as possible."

It was Kitty Hall's turn to gasp. "You two?" she asked.

"Yes." Mike winked at Courtney and held his hand out to her.

"When did this happen?" Kitty Hall managed to ask, obviously scrambling for a good exit line.

"She just asked me." Mike and Courtney began to laugh, and their laughter didn't stop when the perplexed newscaster signed off and the two of them wound up in one another's arms.

"You did that on purpose," Courtney exclaimed when the studio lights were going off and Kitty Hall had expressed her surprised thanks.

"Me?" Mike laughed, pulling her into his arms once more.

"Yes. You decided that you'd embarrass me a little." She kissed the tip of his nose. "You wanted everyone to know that I was the one who proposed."

"A little humility never hurt anyone." He laughed again.

"But my mother was watching the program." She rolled her eyes playfully.

"Yes, and she'll be proud of you for taking matters into your own hands." He looked down at her. "And I don't think she'll mind a bit that you're marrying a policeman."

"I don't think she will, either. But," she hesitated, planting a kiss on his chin, "if you don't want me to lose my job you'll let me go so I can run this over to the paper. Otherwise Mr. Wagner's going to fire me."

"He wouldn't dare. You're selling too many papers for him." He slid his arm around to her side. "Let's go."

As though their declaring their love for one another before thousands of people had been a final release, they ran down the hallway of the television studio, startling anyone who happened to get in their way. They felt wild, free, exuberant. Gone was the fear, the doubt, the denial.

When they got to Mike's car, he abruptly pulled her up beside him. "This is the riskiest thing I've ever done," he said. There was nothing that he longed for more than to crush her lips beneath his.

She touched the corner of his mouth with her finger. "It will be worth the risk. I promise."

Then his strong, sure hands were tangling in her hair, drawing her toward him. His lips captured hers with a fire and an intensity like nothing she'd ever known.

When they parted, their breathing harsh and jagged, their eyes glazed with longing, he gasped. "Oh, Courtney, I love you."

"And I love you, Mike. I always will."

He took her hand as they stood by the car. "As soon as we've stopped by the paper, I want to take you to my house."

"Your house?"

"Yes, I have some things to show you. I don't intend to enter this engagement with any secrets between us."

The way he was smiling at her made her wonder what he had to show her, but she wasn't worried. Now that she had him she intended never to let him go, and there was nothing he could show her that would change her mind about her love.

She ran into the office and hurried down the steps to the pressroom. Her copy was late and she knew it.

"Hi," she said to the weekend shop foreman. "I'm late with this, but the big boss has it laid out already."

"He's approved it finally? He's been calling me every hour on the hour." The man chewed a wet cigar.

"Well, here it is," she said, dashing away from him.

"It's approved, then?" he called after her.

"You'd better get it set, hadn't you?" She kept running.

The last thing she heard was his muttering about overtime and better conditions. She figured he could handle her boss as well as she could. Besides, what she'd written would sell papers. There were plenty of romantics left in San Antonio.

Mike drove straight to his house. When he stopped the car, Courtney sat very still. Then she spoke. "It's a lovely home."

"Thanks. I hope you'll like it."

He led her inside the ranch-style white brick structure. As soon as they entered through the bright red double doors she was standing in an open living area with a vaulted ceiling. There was creamy white carpeting that felt thick beneath her shoes, pastel cushions on the sofa and vividly colored paintings on the wall. Though it was nicer, much larger and more inviting, it still was very similar in style to her apartment.

"It's wonderful," she said.

"Good. I'll show you the rest of it when our business is taken care of." He grabbed her hand and propelled her through the living area, down a skylit corridor and into his bedroom. "Sit down there and make yourself comfortable." He motioned to his bed.

There were louvered doors on one wall. She wondered what was behind them, but she didn't have to wonder long.

He turned on the overhead light, then, for added brightness, switched on the lamp on the bedside table. He went purposefully to the louvered doors and threw them open. Inside were floor-to-ceiling shelves filled with books, albums, framed photographs, and other objects that obviously had special meaning for Mike.

"Where to begin," Mike said, staring up at the shelves. "Okay, I guess we'll start here." He reached up for a photo album that was torn and tattered. "I've had this since I had my first job in the third grade. A neighbor who lived near my foster parents at that time took my picture. You'll see me on the first page. My first out-of-school picture."

Sitting on the edge of the bed, Courtney opened the album he handed her and then stared down at a picture of a little boy. He was a handsome child with a warm smile and big, dark eyes that stared intently out of the photograph.

"When you get tired of looking at the album," he said, "I have other things to show you. My last medical report, my tax returns."

"What are you talking about?" she asked, still not comprehending.

"I'm talking about having no secrets. I'm talking about sharing my life with you. That boy you see there—" he pointed to the photograph in the album "—is what I'm about. Those are my beginnings, my past." He turned the page of the album. "Here's the first dog I ever had, Chip. A Heinz 57. I loved Chip," he said enthusiastically.

He went back to the shelf, picked up a baseball and brought it to her. When she took it he said, "It's from my first game out of the sandlot. Everyone on the team signed it, including the coach. I hit a home run. I had my first taste of victory. I went to college on a scholarship. Baseball did it for me.''

She turned the yellowing ball around in her hand. The signatures were faded, but still legible.

''That meant my future, when I found out I had a knack for pitching. It got me out of having to be dependent on other people. I could go to college and pay my own way.'' He was grinning at the memory. ''You can't know what freedom that represented to me.''

''And after college?''

''After college I decided I had to be a policeman. I wanted the chance to be on the side of right and good. I was idealistic as hell.''

''And you still are,'' she added.

His grin widened. ''Still am.'' He nodded. ''I hope you can live with that.''

''I can't wait,'' she whispered.

He took a step toward her, and bent to brush her lips with his. She reached out for him, but he stepped back.

''No,'' he said softly. ''Not until you've seen everything.''

He went back to his shelves. ''I met Nancy when I was a rookie cop. She was a secretary at the downtown police station. She had a nice smile, and she was very shy. There was something very vulnerable about her. I think now I probably felt sorry for her from the instant I saw her." He handed Courtney a framed photograph of a wistful-looking blonde. "When I got to know her, I found out she was pregnant. Her boyfriend was on the force, but he was already married and he wasn't interested in getting a divorce."

"She's lovely," Courtney told him, trying not to show him her trepidation.

"Yeah. Nice girl. Her baby needed a name, so I married her. I wasn't in love, but I was willing to work at it, and I was tired of being alone. When she gave birth to a little girl I wanted to be the father I'd never had."

"What happened?" she asked cautiously.

"Nancy hated the force, hated the long, unpredictable hours, everything. Her ex-boyfriend finally got a divorce, and she went to Seattle with him." He shook his head. "I try to tell myself it was the best thing for Kara, her daughter. She'd be with her real father that way. Nancy asked me not to see her for a while, to give Kara a chance to get to know her father without me around."

"It must be very difficult."

"Yeah, well—" His voice trailed off to nothing.

"Anyway, that's what happened. Do you want to know my shirt size? Fifteen medium, fifteen and a half. I have my suit measurements here somewhere, too," he said, reaching for yet another book. "Oh, and my bank account. I've managed to save some money.''

"Mike," she said softly, "You don't have to tell me all these things right now. There will be plenty of time for that later.''

"But I want no secrets."

"Your shirt size is no secret. I could have guessed that for myself.''

He laughed. "You know what I mean."

"Yes, I do," she replied, "and I appreciate it all very much. There's only one thing right now, though, that makes any difference to me.''

He came to sit beside her. He looked into her eyes and took her hands in his, caressing her wrists gently.

"What's that?"

"I want to know if you love me, if you want to love me forever.''

He laughed again. His eyes lit up with pleasure. "Is that all you want?"

She nodded.

"Woman, you're too easy. Courtney Evans, I love you. With all my heart, all my soul. For me now there is no past, only the future, and you, my love, are my future.''

"Our love is all that matters," she murmured, hungry to feel his mouth against hers.

"There's one more thing," he cautioned.

"What?" She didn't want to talk anymore. She wanted him to make love to her.

"I vow to always express what's in my heart and in my mind." Slowly he stood and discarded first his jacket, then his tie. Then, one by one, he unfastened the buttons of his shirt.

She couldn't resist the groan that rose from her throat, and her heart fluttered at the way he looked at her as he lay down beside her on the bed. There was trust and openness in his look, and love.

They were never again going to be intimate strangers. They would be together forever. Soul mates. Lovers. Friends.

* * * * *

For the millions who can't read
Give the Gift of Literacy

**One out of five adults in North America
cannot read or write well enough
to fill out a job application
or understand the directions on a bottle of medicine.**

**You can change all this by joining the fight
against illiteracy.**

For more information write to:
Contact, Box 81826, Lincoln, Neb. 68501
In the United States, call toll free: 1-800-228-8813

**The only degree you need
is a degree of caring**

LIT-A-1R

It was a misunderstanding that could cost a young woman her
virtue, and a notorious rake his heart.

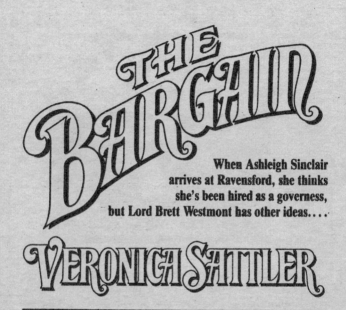

THE BARGAIN

When Ashleigh Sinclair
arrives at Ravensford, she thinks
she's been hired as a governess,
but Lord Brett Westmont has other ideas....

VERONICA SATTLER

Take 4 Silhouette Desire novels
and a surprise gift
❧ FREE ❧

Then preview 6 brand-new Silhouette Desire novels—delivered to your door as soon as they come off the presses! If you decide to keep them, you pay just $2.24 each*—a 10% saving off the retail price, *with no additional charges for postage and handling!*

Silhouette Desire novels are not for everyone. They are written especially for the woman who wants a more satisfying, more deeply involving reading experience. Silhouette Desire novels take you beyond the others.

Start with 4 Silhouette Desire novels and a surprise gift absolutely FREE. They're yours to keep without obligation. You can always return a shipment and cancel at any time.

Simply fill out and return the coupon today!

*$2.25 each plus 69¢ postage and handling per shipment in Canada.

Silhouette ● Desire®

COMING NEXT MONTH

#403 SANTIAGO HEAT—Linda Shaw
When Deidre Miles crash-landed in steamy Santiago, powerful Francis MacIntire saved her from the clutches of a treacherous military. But what could save her from Francis himself, his tumultuous life and flaming desire?

#404 SOMETIMES A MIRACLE—Jennifer West
Bodyguard Cassandra Burke wistfully dreamed of shining knights on white chargers. Cynical ex-rodeo star Alex Montana had long since turned in his steed. As they braved murder and mayhem together, just who would protect whom?

#405 CONQUER THE MEMORIES—Sandra Dewar
For social worker Carla Foster it was time to face the music. In an adoption dispute, Drake Lanning recognized her for the singer she used to be, and he vowed to learn why she hid her talent...and her heart.

#406 INTO THE SUNSET—Jessica Barkley
Lindsay Jordan wasn't just another city slicker playing cowgirl, no matter what ornery stable manager Nick Leighton said. And despite his sensual persuasion, she wasn't greenhorn enough to think of riding off into the sunset with him!

#407 LONELY AT THE TOP—Bevlyn Marshall
Corporate climber Keely LaRoux wasn't about to let maverick photographer Chuck Dickens impede her progress up the ladder. But traveling together on assignment, the unlikely pair found that business could fast become a dangerously addictive pleasure.

#408 A FAMILY OF TWO—Jude O'Neill
Hotshot producer Gable McCrea wanted newcomer Annabel Porter to direct his latest movie. But what inner demons prompted him to sabotage her work... and her growing love for him?

AVAILABLE THIS MONTH:

#397 SOLITAIRE
Lindsay McKenna

#398 LOVE CAN MAKE IT BETTER
Allyson Ryan

#399 A VISION TO SHARE
Jillian Blake

#400 THE MAN BEHIND THE BADGE
Paula Hamilton

#401 SUMMERTIME BLUES
Natalie Bishop

#402 BREAKING EVERY RULE
Victoria Pade